About the Author

Saja Ibrahim was born in the United States, lived and grew up in Saudi Arabia. Her ancestors are of different origins which leaves her exposed to various cultures and traditions. She has done a bachelors in Marketing and studied yoga practice and philosophy. The first novel she read was picked off her grandmother's bed stand when she was a teenager and she hasn't stopped reading since. She writes today in hope that somewhere in her stories we find a way to leave the world a better place than we received it.

In The Wake of Change

Saja Ibrahim

In The Wake of Change

Olympia Publishers
London

www.olympiapublishers.com
OLYMPIA PAPERBACK EDITION

A CIP catalogue record for this title is
available from the British Library.

ISBN: 978-1-80439-346-8

This is a work of fiction.
Names, characters, places and incidents originate from the writer's
imagination. Any resemblance to actual persons, living or dead, is
purely coincidental.

First Published in 2023

Olympia Publishers
Tallis House
2 Tallis Street
London
EC4Y 0AB

Printed in Great Britain

Dedication

To a soul larger than life, my inspiration and support, my Maryam.

In the Wake of Change

Prologue

Life is nothing but a collage of perceptions we create around tangible (people, material and environment) and non-tangible (Soul or Spirit) elements that shape our Universe, a Universe that comes into existence with our awareness and shall disappear with it. In a constant effort to make our lives better we call upon our Universe teachers to guide us through.

Now no one would stand in a class room full of students and try to teach Math except for a Mathematician confident in his mastery in the art of Math. So it makes sense that the teacher of life, of which one of the most important lessons is humility, would be a master humble enough to renounce all form. He shall not dress himself as an accomplished professor available only to the educated, nor sit in a shape of a guru limited to those who have the courage to leave the worldly and seek his presence. He shall not speak as an Imam restricted to a certain faith. He shall not compete with the love of a mother or argue with the protective instinct of a father. The teacher of life, life itself shape shifts possessing all that surrounds us. Sometimes he speaks to us through our professors, gurus and Imams and sometimes through peasants and servants, sometimes through our parents and others through our children. Sometimes he whispers through explosions and others echos in the silence.

These lessons are not meant to be a once in a life time eye opening spectacle. There is no life changing experience or one answer fits all and that's the beauty of it. This teacher continuously guides us through the journey, life holds your hand and walks with you. If a student asks a question a thousand times, the teacher answers a million, but if the student is not listening there is no way they will ever understand.

I invite you to be quiet and listen even if the lesson entails you to let go of all you perceived life to be.

Discipline

I remembered to flinch, stiffened my legs, rubbed my hands on my pants pretending to wipe off sweat. I avoided looking directly at him. "Wait I need a minute," I said, closed my eyes, took a deep breath in through the nose and blew out through my mouth. "Okay I'm ready now."

When he didn't say anything for a while, I looked at him to see what was wrong. "Layla! Why didn't you tell me you've done this before?" he asked with his eyes fixed on my foot that was resting on the brake pedal.

"It was a long time ago when I was just a kid, my cousins took me driving in America one summer," I spurted out my backup lie.

"Fine. Drive." He rested his arms behind his head like he always did when he was upset. I drove us back home, a smooth twenty minute drive with no mistakes and we buried that incident with all the other unspoken conversations we chose to forget about.

Ever since we spotted our first female driver on the road and up to that day this man never failed to let out a comment like "I wonder who taught her how to drive?"

"Look how she's making that U-turn, she blocked the whole street."

He would speed up to a bad driver just to prove to me that it was a woman behind the wheel.

"Don't sit by the entrance when you get to the coffee

shop, the other day I saw a woman drive right into a store" he repeatedly warned me before showering me with grand gestures like "I'm thinking of buying a cheap used car for the driver to run his personal errands, you can drive it too".

So forgive me for being a little reluctant to tell him, my husband of fifteen years, that I drove around in a Z8 when I was nineteen.

I grew up in a beautiful three story house circling around a garden with a fountain in the middle. The hallways on each floor had big glass windows looking into the garden and consequently into each other, a perfect design by my grandfather to bring the family together. He did not need to ask us to join him on his evening walks, all he had to do was put on his shorts and shoes and walk toward the door slow enough for us to catch him. We walked to a small shop at the end of the street. He gave me and my two siblings five Riyals each to buy candy. He allowed us to jump on his bed, ride our bikes and play with water guns inside the house. "The maids clean every day, what's an extra stain or two," he told anyone who tried to stop us. He dropped us to school and allowed us to skip whenever we faked a stomach ache. He hid us in his office for the rest of the day, where we watched him rule. To most people this tall, strong and loud man with eyes widely bulging out to the future was a source of intimidation. For me my grandfather, my dada, was my backbone, my strength.

My favorite memories were of the holidays. Ramadan, was either a full thirty days month, or cut short depending on the moon. We all sat in front of the TV on the evening of the twenty ninth and waited for the newsman to confirm the sighting of a new moon and when he didn't, we repeated this the next day. All though it was a given, we did not celebrate until he made the announcement that tomorrow was Eid. We jumped to our feet, squeezed each other and with an eruption of mixed emotions uttered the words Eid Mubarak. We were parting with the disciplined life we adopted for a whole month. For a whole month we interrupted our sleep an hour before sunrise so we could fill our stomachs and drink a last sip of water. We raced against the days trying to finish reading the Quran, stood on our prayer mats until late hours of the night asking Allah to forgive the sins weighing us down and those we were yet to commit. We silently gathered around an eighteen seater dining table ten minutes before sunset. Everyone, guests and all had to be present before my grandfather unless we wanted to give him a reason to lash out. Diabetes and High Blood Pressure were to blame for his short temper and no matter how quiet we were he would break a glass, throw a plate or insult a nephew. We the grandkids found this show funny and he always spotted that hidden smile behind our eyes. His lips pierced, his face turned red, his belly and shoulders shook up and down then we all laughed. My grandmother sitting to his right pretended he was invisible. A technique I later used with my kids when they threw tantrums and I did not want to encourage bad behavior. There was something magical about that dining table, no one could stay mad for long. No matter how upset two people were at each other, the respect we had for my grandmother and the fear of my grandfather made one meal enough for reconciliation. Then that life ended. We spent the night before Eid washing the windows and floors, changing our bedsheets and towels, donating old clothes and making room for everything new.

On mornings when we didn't have school I helped my grandmother, Dadi, water plants, shine silver and clean lentils. She then shooed me away so she could watch the news and read Quran. She spent her afternoons working on a jigsaw puzzle and evenings watching TV and crocheting. She waited for us with a fruit platter and popped slices of apple and pears into our mouths as she caught us up on her series. She turned every meal into a special occasion. We all had our assigned spots in front of our favorite dishes. Like a hotel lobby, people stopped at our house at any given time for a light bite, a quick venting session and some over dramatic conspiracy.

Dadi had a presence that filled the room with a strange calm. You could come to her with the biggest troubles in life and instantly they disappeared. She would take one look at your eyes and quietly place your head on her lap, run her fingers through your hair and wrap you where nothing could harm you.

She never stepped out of her bedroom in anything less than elegance. When she was a little younger she draped herself in the most beautiful flowing Saris and gracefully aged into delicate cotton Kaftans. For as long as anyone remembered she had glowing skin and thick lashes and never wore make up. She had gentle eyes and a subtle smile that didn't leave her lips not even on the day I accidentally saw Dada hit her. He did not know I was in the kitchen; he would never do anything like that in front of me.

I watched her boil milk for her tea and mustered the courage to ask why she tolerated him? Why didn't she just leave? Was it because she had nowhere else to go?

"Tauba Tauba! We don't leave people because they are broken." She asked me to sit down and began to tell me a story.

"I married your grandfather when I was fourteen. With tears in their eyes, my family placed me on a palanquin that carried me to school every day, only that day I was wearing a red Sari embroidered with threads made out of real gold and being escorted to your Dada's house where I was welcomed with a loud celebration. My name was no longer Ama the princess of mischief, I became Mrs. Ibrahim and I was no longer carried around on palanquins. I carried trays of food and tea and shortly after, a baby.

One day religion exploded and divided our country. Your grandfather saved me. He did everything he could so your father and I wouldn't witness the horrors that were happening around us. He spent the night covering windows, not in blackout but with beautiful Iranian rugs. He made sandwiches and filled a flask with tea, your grandfather never made tea in his life, it was bad. He did it because he did not want me to go to the kitchen near the entrance. He assigned two of his strongest cousins to guard the door and took the first train to Delhi. He went to sell our house to a friend, the house he spent seven years of sweat building. His friend placed cash and the legal documents to facilitate our departure in a brief case with his Hindu name carved on the leather because it was all he could find. On your Dada's way back, his train was attacked by the Hindus. He got scared and hid his face behind the briefcase. They saw the name, spared him and slaughtered everyone else. He stepped on corpses, stumbled and fell in blood several times. Just around the corner from our house he came face to face with the Muslims who saw him carrying a brief case with a Hindu name and swung a knife across his stomach. You know that scar he always shows you claiming he got from fighting a tiger?"

"Yeah," I said as I watched her let out a giggle and quickly come back to her story.

"His childhood friend Mehmood recognized him and stopped them from killing him. He took him to a doctor and cleaned him up before bringing him home. I only know this because his cousin came over for Hajj years later and told me. He also told me that your dada's parents called him a coward, accused him of abandoning them and his country, they told him that if he left they would not want to see his face again not even on the day of their burial.

Dada wrapped me and your father in a blanket, he held our faces against his body, occasionally asked us to cover our ears and hummed loudly so all we could hear was the calming sound of his vibrating heart. we were only allowed to look when we landed in Jeddah. This man of men broke himself to pieces so he could protect me.

I was no longer Mrs. Ibrahim of my district, I was a poor woman granted refuge in the land of god. Dada worked day and night built a name for himself and surrounded me with people who treat me like a queen.

My passport no longer said Hindustan on the cover, it said Saudi Arabia and it doesn't matter because we never went back to bury our parents.

I learnt to let go of my home, my family, my name and my nationality, things I never expected to be taken away from me. My body however, I always knew I was bound to leave behind some day. If your Dada believes he can get back some of himself by pushing it around, so be it."

I figured the only way to protect my grandmother from my grandfather was to shadow her throughout the day. So I glued myself to her as soon as I returned from school which was usually before Dada came back from work. I pretended to develop some sort of night terror and demanded she, not my mother, sleep with me. With time my grandparents eased themselves apart, she moved into a separate bedroom and my father fixed one of the living rooms on the middle floor just for her. I promised myself I would never be victimized by a man like Dada and for that I needed to become him. I needed an intellect that earned me a deadly stare and biceps that allowed me to stop a raised hand so I buried myself in my books and befriended my dumbbells through high school.

Three long years of stress related acne and split ends later, I ran to my mother with the newspaper that listed the names of high school graduates with my name somewhere on the top. I told her I wanted to apply for colleges abroad, she shrugged and said I could go when I was married. "But Mama!"

"No! Your elder brother didn't even ask to go. Get married and you can go with your husband."

That was the most ridiculous thing I had ever heard. One of five children, my mother was so used to deprivation and sacrifice her first response to anything was no. Because life was unfair and you could not have everything you want, and the sooner she taught me that the better. But there was no way for me to understand where she was coming from at such a young age, I hated her for being so strict. My father on the other hand, son of such a strong personality, I resented for his passiveness and weak presence.

I settled for business school in Jeddah and I'm glad I did for if I hadn't, I never would have met my best friend Hala. Hala came back home with me after classes every Thursday and every Thursday she begged my mother to allow me to go with her family to the beach on Friday. One day Hala's Mom called mine and told her she was offended that she would not trust them enough to send me. "If your daughter can't come to us then I'm not sending my daughter to your house anymore," she said. From then on, I spent occasional Fridays at Hala's family's beach house. It was a private compound with eight small huts where everyone knew each other so naturally I, the incoming stranger, got much attention. I smiled at the staring women and pretended not to notice the men who never stopped. One day my friend explained to me why. "You're prettier than you think you are. We all believe it must be the mixed blood you carry inside you." I loved spending time at the beach with Hala and her free-spirited family. They were all so very joyful and loud and welcomed me like I had been born into them. They introduced me to different music, hairstyles and makeup and up to this day each and every one of them is an extension of my family.

We sat at the pier, someone I had never seen before parked his jet ski at arm's reach from me and stepped away for a moment. I felt my soul being pulled out of the depths of my body and the entire existence blurred out behind a drop of water. When he hopped back on his jet ski, it tilted to the right almost flipping him over. I held it down with my leg, grabbed his hand and pulled him back to balance. "Thank you," he said with a big smile. I shyly looked away.

In the evening when everyone went inside to freshen up, I was left out alone as usual. I did not want to impose, so I always waited for the men in Hala's family to come back outside before I stepped in. He limped toward me, not because there was something wrong with his leg, but because it was some cool gangster thing guys like him used to do. "I'm Abdullah. You're a very strong girl," he said as he shook my hand, looked me in the eye, said his phone number just once then walked away. We must have had super memory powers back then for I still remember those nine digits in proper order. As soon as I got back home I locked my bedroom door and called him. He didn't answer, he waited for me to hang up then called me back. "Just leave me a missed call anytime and I'll call you right back. I don't want to get you in trouble." Because back then calling someone on their cell phone cost one Riyal per minute, a text message was one or two Riyals depending on its length and at the end of the month your parents received a detailed invoice with numbers, time and duration.

Abdullah, a gorgeously masculine man, borrowed out of a dream as Hala had put it, spent hours on the phone with me and on Friday we watched each other across the crowd, making notes in our head of the things we wanted to say later. One day he called me from a landline. "Hang up and call me back on this number, okay?"

"But why?"

"Quickly. Bye." He hung up. I dialed the number from my landline and said hello to the strange voice on the other end.

"Salam Alaikum, may Allah grant you a long life. I will transfer your call right away," the man said in a very respectful manner.

"Who was that?" I nervously asked Abdullah.

"The operator, now you can call me here anytime. And now he knows to put you through or find me."

"How many people live in your house?"

"Four, my parents, my brother and I."

"Why do you need an operator?" I teased him.

"Am Salem (Uncle Salem a former driver of theirs from Sudan) is too old to do anything else."

Landline to landline was free and untraceable. Still, dialing his home number was such a bizarre privilege I never dared to try.

Abdullah and I fell into each other's habits, we woke each other up with kisses on the phone, he got ready for work and I for college. We talked until I reached class. He planned his meetings around my breaks so we could sneak in a few more conversations. He changed the day he got together with his friends from Wednesday to Thursday because that was when my family gathered at my grandmother's house for dinner, and I couldn't call him so it made sense he keep Wednesdays free and we both were occupied on Thursday.

I made myself available to talk to him on his drive back from work, reminded him to wear his seatbelt and secretly said a prayer to protect him on the road.

I skipped summer vacation at London with my parents and siblings to be near him. I always asked for his permission before I left home and let him know I reached my destination safely. Not because I had to but because it was cute. We spoke through the night until one of us fell asleep.

When I was in my second year of college there was an outbreak of nice local and franchised coffee shops across Jeddah. There was a new shopping mall coming up in every other district with brand names we were used to seeing only when we travelled. It was around that time when my mother decided to go out and enjoy life with or without my father. I passed on every opportunity to go with her because her absence gave me more time on the phone with Abdullah.

Other than the beach, Tahlia Street was the easiest and most accessible place for girls and boys to meet.

There were three ways to do so. Option one: a girl would drive up and down the street (her parent's driver would drive with her in the back seat) until she was spotted by an interested boy who followed her long enough for them to get a good look at each other. Most of the time this action was caught by other boys who figured the girl must be quite a catch for the poor fellow to be following her for so long. They would join in and initiate a competition. The girl, somewhat afraid and very much ecstatic with the number of followers, pointed at the person she wanted, and all the others left gracefully. This method was very risky, for Tahlia was a main road and chances of you being seen by a family member were very high. Also if you or your driver weren't skilled enough you could have gotten into an ugly accident. So this was a method used by boys and girls only on days they felt extra reckless.

Option two: a girl would pretend to be driving to a store (again, her parent's driver would be the one doing all the driving). Tahlia was also a main shopping district with your average affordable international brands escalating into more expensive department stores on one side. On the other side was a grand display of high end luxury brands and jewelry boutiques. The girl would take a route long enough for a boy she approves of to spot her. Then she would step into the store with him at her tail. They would get a better look at each other, height, shoes and all. Then she would discreetly take his number and they would respectfully leave the scene if lucky enough, forever.

Option three: Wednesday afternoons at a restaurant we called The Place. Like all other restaurants at the time The Place was segregated into an all men Single's section and a Family section you were only allowed to enter with a female companion. Boys used their sisters, cousins and friends for this purpose. This was a more laid back setting where anyone could sit and talk to anyone. They ate together and met many times before the need to express their interest in one and other.

I avoided Tahlia because I was in a relationship with Abdullah. Until one day when Hala decided to take a detour on our way home. Abdullah was standing in a corner surrounded by some six friends. I was in a moving car, yet our eyes did not fail to catch each other. I nervously answered his call. "What are you doing here?" he yelled at me. I looked at Hala who heard him too.

"I need shampoo." She pointed to a supermarket next to us and said loud enough for him to realize she was part of the conversation and willing to be held accountable.

"Park by that closed store in front of you," he said and hung up before I had a chance to say okay. A few minutes later his friends were lined up in front of Hala's window a different shampoo bottle in each hand. She picked one. "Anything else?" he asked.

"Gum," she jokingly answered.

"Go home." He tapped on the top of the car like he was petting an obedient child. I received a message from him: *My lady doesn't go to supermarkets* and from then on, he always delivered my groceries home for me.

Minus a signature and witnesses, I was married to Abdullah. I knew what it felt like to have my hand in his. I recognized the smell he left hanging in the air. I knew what it was like to be safe in someone's presence. I knew I could rely on him to show up if I ever got in trouble, to listen to me whine when I had a fever and humor me when I was PMSing. I had him to share a laugh at bad jokes and contain my unexplained tears. I knew what it felt like to have the kind of authority over someone that allowed you to demand unreasonable sacrifices just because.

While I was floating around in a romantic bubble, I overheard my aunt and mother discuss which shade of lipstick would make my father more jealous. I realized my mother had not been going out and about just for fun but rather in a desperate call for my father's attention, who was busy reading reports and watching movies. I felt sorry for her and decided to invite her into my bubble.

Abdullah and his friends were playing the Oud and singing her favorite song by Abadi Aljohar. I ran to her room and nervously looked at her lying there staring at the ceiling fan. I pulled myself together, hopped next to her on the bed and put him on speaker. She enjoyed the song while it lasted, then asked me, "Who is that?" with something other than the fascination I was aiming for piercing into my soul.

"His name is Abdullah Alzahrani, you will love him," I

emphasized on her favorite type of music and the Saudi tribal last name. For although my grandparents and father had been Saudi Nationals since long before I was born, my father held on to his heritage. My mother's family on the other hand, were locals who never failed at any given occasion to make a racist comment against my father's origin. I always believed she would be happier if I married a full-fledged Saudi.

"Where did you meet him?"

"At the beach."

"So they have a beach house?"

"Yes."

"You know they only marry from the same tribe, and if he does marry you, they will always look down at us. Why would you put me and your father through so much humiliation?"

I cried.

"Did you go out with him?"

"No."

"A thousand thanks to Allah. Listen to me, boys who call girls on their phone only want to take advantage of them and once they get what they want, they leave them. Besides, Zuneira and Ali are coming to propose for their son Essa next week."

"What? No!"

"What do you mean no? You said you wanted to study abroad? He is studying in London and wants to take you with him."

I cried.

"Listen to me I am your mother, no one loves you more than I do and I will always want what's best for you," then came the last draw "Beridaya Alaiki" (a mother's Rida, her satisfaction was a gateway to heaven. If we failed to satisfy our mothers at whom's feet lay heaven, we would not be allowed to enter. This was a lesson we had been repeatedly taught since kindergarten and now leaving Abdullah was the price).

I ended things with Abdullah and fell on the floor with my back against the door where I cried my lungs out, hoping my mother would hear me and make it hurt a little less.

On Friday, my father came back from the mosque and summoned me to the living room where he gave me his very first piece of advice. "Ali and Zuneira are coming over tonight with a marriage proposal. Did Essa say anything to you?"

"No."

"He wants to marry you."

"But I don't want to marry him."

"What's this nonsense? Is there someone else?"

"No."

"Then you will behave yourself tonight. They're our old friends and we will not disrespect them."

"But I don't love him."

"Love has nothing to do with marriage. He is a decent boy, marry him, go get yourself a good degree and if you still can't live with him get a divorce."

A cousin helped me put on a long peach dress and soft makeup. I sat in the middle of one room with all the women sipping coffee and trying to figure out how they might be distantly related. The men gathered in another room, raised their hands to the sky and recited Surat Al Fatiha. My brother knocked on the door with the news that I was engaged, the women let out ullulis, kissed and hugged each other and me. Then everyone except me, his mother, sisters and aunts covered their hair and allowed Essa in.

He sat next to me. Essa, someone who I had known since childhood without asking how I was doing, pulled a ring out of his pocket, reached for my hand and slid it on my finger. Later that night, I took off the ring that did not look like anything I would ever pick out of a jewelry store and called Abdullah.

"What happened?" he asked.

"I'm engaged," I said with tears choked up my throat.

"Listen to me, I love you too much to allow you to disrespect yourself like this and please don't make a dishonorable man out of me. You will be happy give him a chance."

I cried.

"Remember I can't ever stop loving you even if I try," he said then hung up.

I cried myself to sleep and woke up to my ringing phone. "Hello," I said without looking at the screen.

"Hi." It wasn't Abdullah waking me up it was Essa.

"Congratulations we're engaged," he said.

"Yes, congratulations."

"Are you happy Layla?" Finally someone asked me.

"Are you happy?" I asked him.

"Very! I've been waiting for this day since you were only sixteen, I confided in my sister and we decided we should wait. I wanted you to live your life to the fullest before being in a commitment. Your parents always spoke of how ambitious you are. I quit my job and went to London so I too could have a college degree and make you proud. We will have the wedding in time for you to join me next semester. You don't need to worry about a thing. I will take care of the paper work and find us a nice place to stay. I will wait for you to study for as long as you want then we can come back home. Oh my god, listen to me blabbering! Are you late for class?"

"Yes."

"I'll pick you up later, we can grab dinner before my flight."

"Okay."

He took me to a fancy Japanese Restaurant. I was embarrassed to be seen with him alone in public and a little surprised my mother allowed it. A group of women stared at us as we held hands and followed a waiter to a corner table covered with candles and red roses. I was too upset to look at Essa and wanted to avoid the women so I watched a family sitting on our right.

The father must have been somewhere in his fifties, the mother in her late thirties and two teenage boys. I admired how the man allowed his hand to rest under hers while he struggled to do everything with just his left. Between sipping on her soup, the woman looked up at her men and around with a proud spark in her eyes. I convinced myself that maybe god was giving me a glimpse of what a future with Essa would look like and it wasn't bad at all.

I had been to that restaurant with my parents on my mother's birthday and knew what I wanted to order. Dumplings and prawn in sweet chili sauce, but before I could say anything the waiter started to serve us duck wraps and Saudi Champagne. Like a magician pulling out surprises from his hat at a children's birthday party, Essa surprised me with a different gift bag every five minutes. He then started to rant about a future he had spent the last two years planning with an imaginary me.

This sweet soul that I liked since childhood and may have had a crush on at some point in my life was suffocating me. I was tied to a rock and he was pulling me down a river. The waiter brought out our main dish, Wagyu beef and noodles. I did not like noodles, they made some really good vegetable fried rice there.

But I couldn't hurt Essa's feelings, clearly he had planned this night up to the moment where diamond ear rings popped out of his pocket. Diamond ear rings that matched my engagement ring. He put them on my ears and whispered, "Three more months my love and you will never have to spend a minute away from me."

Essa left for London and I woke up with six missed calls from Abdullah. I was happy to see he thought about me but I was still engaged. Essa called me at eight every evening, we spoke for some fifteen minutes where he updated me in speed about his day and briefly asked me about mine.

His mother invited me to a different gathering every weekend, where she showed me off to all her friends. She snuck in hints to our wedding date and venue but made sure that the confirmation would only be revealed on the invitation cards.

The rock kept getting heavier and the river deeper and faster until I had no choice but to scream for my life. "Essa, I can't do this anymore!"

"Do what?"

"Please try to understand, you've been living a love story for two years without me and you expect me to dive in. I can't keep up, I'm drowning"

"It's okay, I know what's wrong with you."

What? Wait what's wrong with me?

"What's wrong with me?" I snapped.

"It's your parent's fault, their loveless marriage scares you. You don't know how to love."

What the hell was he talking about? The only reason I was marrying him was to make my parents happy and he had the audacity to insult them like that. I hung up and never spoke to him again. I don't know what he told his parents or what they told mine but a couple of days later my mother marched the corridors screaming and yelling, she barged into my bedroom and took my phone away. She refused to speak to me for the next six weeks until my grandmother, her mother, pointed out that marriage was a bond decided by Allah, if it was meant to be no one could find a way to object and if it wasn't, no force in the Universe could make it happen.

I was allowed baby steps back into my freedom. I went to my mother, told her I was bored. When in truth I needed her help before I relapsed. Having my phone in my hands was hard for me. I did not want to betray her trust again. I didn't want to call Abdullah. I asked her if she could take me out on a drive or to get some ice cream. "I'm going out with your aunt," she said.

"But please, Mama," I cried.

"Not today, maybe some other time."

If only my parents could see that I loved them enough to sacrifice love itself, if only they could see that I loved them enough to get married just so they could honor a friendship, if only they could see I would break a finger that dares to point at them even if breaking that finger meant breaking Essa's heart.

Allowed With A Sting

Friday evenings, my parents hosted Carrom night, the women dressed in fancy long gowns and colored head scarfs and the men in casual pants and shirts. They gathered around a two meter wide Carrom board my father had custom made for the occasion. They laughed, joked, played music and sang under dim chandelier lights.

I snuck upstairs, locked my bedroom door and called Abdullah twenty times to tell him my engagement was over, and I was all his again. I left him twenty missed calls every day for the next two weeks. He did not answer.

Protocol was you leave someone no more than three missed calls if they don't call back in twenty-four hours, you respect their choice to move on. Abdullah left me six, I didn't call back until seven months later. I fell to the ground cried my lungs out again and banged my head against the door. I hated that I allowed myself to become this weak and pathetic woman I promised myself I would never be. Not because of a man.

I called Hala and said, "Can you take me to Tahlia?"

Hala dominated Tahlia Street, the mediocre guys knew their place and stayed away from her Maroon Lexus. The stubborn brats raised to believe they could have anything they wanted came back every time, in hope that they could one day get that cool girl with wild curls and a loud giggle. Little did they know that this girl who snuck romantic novels into Calculus class and cried at the end of a book had herself reserved for a more magical encounter and only ventured on Tahlia to feed her confidence. She smiled at a boy in a Mustang. He rolled his window down and yelled, "Will you take my number today?"

"Maybe." She gave him false hope.

She saw that I was confused and gave me my first real lesson in Business: Positioning. "We will keep him hooked until we lure a bigger fish. If you choose to befriend a big fish great! And if you choose a smaller one he will forever know your value." A minute in, we had a White Ferrari by her window, the Mustang found his way to my side and there was a Blue Porsche tailing us. I noticed our driver was getting agitated and got scared.

"Hala, if you're going to take someone's number can you do it already. I need to get out of the car," I said to my friend who was too busy dancing and waving to hear me. A boy in a worn out GMC drove by and looked back to see what all the fuss was about. His disappointed face made me laugh. The Mustang who had been trying to grab my attention for the last five minutes caught me laughing with this guy and sped off to try his luck elsewhere.

We pulled up next to the GMC at a traffic light, he avoided looking at me for a few seconds then smiled and pointed at himself asking if I wanted his number. I shrugged my shoulders shyly, he discreetly held up fingers and I saved his number on my phone. Hala's mission was accomplished. We went back home. I waited until the urge to call Abdullah became unbearable, that is when I called the number. His name was Hamza. "Why me?" he asked. "Why not the guy in the Mustang, the Ferrari or the

Porsche?"

"Why not you?" I answered.

"Because I can't give you the things they would be able to."

"Hamza this is not a marriage proposal." I laughed.

"But if this works out, we will get married," he whined.

I spoke to him for a whole week, he lay out all his insecurities. He came to the mall so I could see how short and chubby he was, he told me how he lived in an apartment with his parents, how that apartment only had window units and not central air-conditioning. He told me how he could not afford to buy me diamonds then said, "Can I ask you for something Layla?"

"Order me," I said with complete submission.

"Please cover your hair when you go out."

"Why?"

"You are so beautiful no man can resist falling in love with you."

"And they won't fall in love with me if they don't see my hair?"

"That's not what I meant."

"I have a better plan; you love me enough that I can't see anyone else."

Hamza loved me enough to cry when I got upset over silly things. He loved me enough to call me twenty times a day. He didn't care if it was fifty degrees outside, he stood under the burning sun just so he could catch a glimpse of me walking across a window in hope that I might see him too. He loved me so much, I'm sure if he loved me anymore he would have exploded.

"I've been calling you for the last thirty minutes, why

didn't you answer?" he asked with a new found confidence.

"I was at the supermarket."

"Why didn't you tell me I could have got you what you needed?" I hung up and ignored his calls long enough for him to give up.

Next, was the boy in the Blue Porsche. Motaz told me he was studying in Boston and was in town to attend a board meeting at his father's company which he would be handling eventually. He was fun, lighthearted, made me laugh like I had never before.

One night around three a.m. my cell phone ran out of battery and he called the house. My mother picked up, he hung up and called again. She picked up again and again until he snapped, "Old woman, why do you keep answering? Clearly I'm not calling for you!" She laughed and allowed me to answer the next time.

A few days later, I ran into my cousin at The Place and told him about this cool boy I had met.

"Motaz doesn't study in Boston! He's a senior at my school, which makes him two years younger than you," he laughed.

"Are you sure?"

Just as my cousin was describing his blond hair, average height and the small scar on his forehead, Motaz called and asked me where I was and if I wanted to go for a drive.

"You're going to live a long life, I was just talking about you," I said.

"Really? With whom?"

"Why aren't you at school?"

"What?"

"It's your graduation year, you can't mess up"

"I'm sorry, you probably never want to speak to me again," he said nervously.

"Why?"

"Because I lied!"

"Motaz, those things you told me about yourself, are they things you want to do and believe you might in the future?"

"Yes."

"Then, that is also you. Right? Just in a different time."

"I hope that when I am all of that, I find you again."

"Why not now?"

"Because if I have you now, I would be less motivated to become that man," he said before he disappeared.

Then there was a medical student I went to meet in the hospital cafeteria. He held my hand and examined my forearm. "What color are you?"

"What?"

"Your skin tone, I've never seen anything like it."

"Brown," I snapped.

"No. Look there's a tint of pink too," he said as his dilated pupils almost sunk into my tanned arm.

I was intrigued by him, someone in the most important of places, studying to handle one of the heaviest responsibilities in the Universe who could blow all life's seriousness away in a puff. Hala did not like where that was headed and quickly intervened. She introduced me to a twenty-nine year old who had just come back from California with a Master's degree. Son of a man who owned half the city was still figuring out what he wanted to do. In the meantime, he dressed like a Shaikh. A date with him was a fusion of western hip-hop and authentic Arabic poetry. He took me to nice restaurants, asked me to slow dance in public and kissed my forehead. Still my soul never left my body to run to him.

My mother caught me in action many times. She confiscated my phone, grounded me for weeks and barged into my room in a prayer cloak repeating verses of exorcism. I apologized and promised I would never let her down again. A few days later I begged for her attention, she ignored me again. Eventually, I grew numb to her threats and gave up on trying to please her and she grew tired of me.

"What?" I asked Hala when I saw her watching me on the phone with someone new.

"It amazes me how much love you still manage to give."

"I don't love him."

"You love him enough to pretend to love him. That must qualify for something."

I put my phone on silent and threw it in my bag. I did not think to look at it until the next afternoon and found a missed call from Abdullah. I called him right away.

"What were you doing in Tahlia yesterday?" he asked without a hello.

"Turning every man I meet into a Abdullah."

"What? Why?" He giggled.

"Because maybe if I had you a hundred times and left you a hundred times I would stop wanting you."

"And have you? Stopped wanting me?"

"Yes." I couldn't possibly go back to Abdullah after betraying him so many times.

"Layla I want you to know that for me you will always be up there with the moon and stars."

"And for me you'll be right here filling every corner of my soul, and still it will long for you." I knew then that was the last time he would ever reach out to me.

Hala and I stopped going to Tahlia, we found a new place to hang out. A small cafe/restaurant near her house that served Argeela. Hala smoked because she believed it was cool. I smoked because with every puff I imagined myself disappear into thin air. We spent hours at that cafe every chance we got. One day the thinning smoke revealed a face. He smiled at me for less than a second then looked away before the people on his table noticed. They were a party of five, three men and two women clearly there on business. I could tell from the women's plain black abayas, their properly covered hair and straight backs against chairs slightly pulled away from the table keeping them at a comfortable distance from the men. How they flashed their expensive watches and diamond wedding rings. Their discussion became louder as they threw around big numbers then fell into a subtle agreement.

Hala and I ran out of conversations and quietly enjoyed each other's presence. She burnt her Argeela out and came to a jump. "I need cigarettes."

"You can have my Argeela," I said.

"No my head is pounding, I need a cigarette." She called her driver to fetch her a pack from a close by store and impatiently waited for him by the entrance. When she came back, she waved a business card in my face and I laughed at how silly she could be.

"It's for you. It's from the guy who was sitting over

there, he wanted me to give it to you."

"No, it's okay. You can call him," I mumbled.

"Why would I do that? Call him. He's a little older but cute from up close. Trust me."

She put the card on the table and pushed it toward me. I threw it in my bag and ordered my favorite four cheese pasta and French fries.

My parents were out of town for a week and my siblings busy with their friends. I spent some time with my grandmother then headed to my room. The silence made it hard for me to breath, I dialed Hala but remembered she was busy at a family dinner so I didn't wait for her to answer. I muffled through my bag for the business card and called Raed.

"Hi," he didn't even wonder who I was.

"What took you so long?" he asked.

"I wasn't going to call, it was a little rude what you did."

"What did I do now?"

"You can't give a girl your number to pass on to another girl."

"Shit! Was she upset?"

"Probably, but she wouldn't say."

"I'm sorry, but I had to leave and she was right there by the door. And I knew that your eyes would keep me up all night if I didn't at least try." We stayed quiet for a while then he said, "Can I ask you something?"

"Yes."

"How bad does it hurt?"

"Does what hurt?"

"The pain in your eyes."

"There's no pain my eyes," I laughed.

"There's nothing but pain in your eyes," he said then asked, "Was it a guy?"

"Yeah."

"I recently got divorced I have a six year old son."

"I'm sorry, what happened?"

"Well by the time I admitted to all the things I was doing wrong it was too late to undo them. What did your guy do?"

"Nothing."

"Then why did you leave him?"

"My mother pulled the Beridaya Alaiki card. And by the time I found him again I had lost his Layla somewhere."

Raed and I shared books, movies and family gossip. He called me when he picked his son up from school so I could hear his cute voice. We brought each other gifts when we came back from vacations and on birthdays.

He picked me up from college and we went for ice cream, coffee or a quick lunch. He drove next to me on days my mother decided to keep a tighter watch and accompany the driver and texted me *Smile.*

One Monday, he drove me out to Obhur, a district near the beach busy on weekends but deserted during the week. He stopped the car and stepped out. "Come, your turn to drive." He opened my door and offered me his hand.

"Are you serious? I can't drive."

"Why not?"

"Well, I don't know how to, and this is Saudi Arabia we could get caught."

"I'm right here, you don't need to worry about things like that with me by your side."

"But still."

"If someone stops us, I am teaching you to drive because you are leaving town and we're doing it in the middle of nowhere so we are not trying to defy the law. Okay?"

"What if I scratch your car."

"I'll take it to the workshop, come on now. That's the brake and that's the gas, be gentle." He flattened the back of his seat, closed his eyes and said, "Go now, the world is yours."

Raed and I drove around in his Z8, while singing our lungs out to Broken by Seether almost every week and it didn't matter who was behind the wheel.

"I'm really nervous about the interview tomorrow," I told him when the song ended.

"You'll do great, don't worry and if it doesn't go well I can make some calls."

"What do you think they'll ask me?"

"Well they might ask you where you see yourself in five years, what your strengths and weaknesses are?"

"I don't know what my strengths and weaknesses are?"

"Sure you do, your strength is that you can make any idiot of a man believe he is king of the world."

"Haha, yeah and what's my weakness?"

"You forget that it was you who made him."

When my interviewer leaned back and asked with a big smile, "What would you say is your greatest strength and what is your weakness"

I answered, "Numbers, I'm good with numbers"

"And your weakness?"

"I get bored easily."

"Would that be a problem? What if you get bored working here?"

"Luckily if I'm part of your Marketing team it would be my job to make sure no employee gets bored working here." He handed me a written offer on my way out. I nailed my dream job in a beautiful office building where I could see the beach from my cubicle.

When my brother graduated two years before me, my grandfather showered him with gifts and my parents threw a big dinner party. I'm not sure they even know I graduated. My father never saw my certificate and my mother came by my office just to make sure the females sat in a separate space than the males. Instead of noticing the important context of my phone calls she listened carefully just so she could condemn my tone of voice too feminine for a professional conversation.

Having a job introduced me to me, to what it was like to be passionately driven down a road that led to no one but myself. My victories were my doing and so were my failures and I celebrated both equally.

A few years later, I met my husband.

When I look back at that time I had with Raed, I imagine him walking me down the aisle, helping me mute out the voices of all the men I broke sitting on one side of the isle, yelling a collective curse "May your heart never be full" and turning a blind eye to the scrutinizing faces of my family sitting on the other side waiting for me to mess up.

At the end, one step away from my future husband Saeed, we had the inevitable conversation.

"So this is it?" Raed said with a sigh.

"Unless you want to marry me," I answered.

"I don't think either one of us would be happy if that happened."

"True."

"It was fun loving you without the messy part."

"It was fun loving you too without the messy part, bye." I said between tears and smiles.

In 2018 women were permitted to drive in Saudi Arabia. Not only were they allowed to drive, they were also allowed to label men as friends and colleagues, meet them for coffee or dinner. They were allowed to sit in a living room surrounded by their family and text these men while staring straight into their parent's eyes. They were allowed to stamp red hearts and leave public comments on each other's pictures.

I met Raed in 2002 and spoke to him last before I got married in 2005. My husband decided it was time for me to learn how to drive somewhere in 2020.

I was still not allowed to so much as know if Raed was alive. There was never any law against it, but now only half the nation was exempt from our long taught values while the other half was still obliged to carry them. Not to pass or impose them on to a next generation but just carry them.

In 2022, in the midst of a conversation with Hala I confessed that it wasn't Raed the person that I missed, it was the relationship itself. Hala, who had a driving license and was the most incredible friend a human could ask for, rented a convertible, played some loud music and allowed me to drive us to a coffee shop.

A mid aged conservative Saudi woman in a beige Abaya and off-white scarf over her head sat on a table next to us. She was joined by a blond younger man, given his accent most likely European. She ordered a cappuccino. He ordered a black coffee and a club sandwich. It disturbed me that he did not ask her if she wanted to eat anything.

"So, I wanted to ask, did you feel oppressed growing up in a country where you were only recently allowed to drive?" He leaned into her and said loud enough for everyone to hear.

"Why would I have felt oppressed?"

"Not being able to drive?"

"Well, if I was oppressed because I could not drive myself to college then what of the eighteen year old who has to run under the rain carrying her portfolio to catch a bus. The girl who most likely has to work an evening shift to afford a weekly pass on that bus. We couldn't afford a driver when I was growing up, my father, then my brother drove me to school. It gave my brother a sense of responsibility and I felt cared for. You know up to this day my brother calls me every day to ask me if I need him to bring me anything. I'm married, I have a driver to do my groceries, and have my own car but still he would ask.

For the less fortunate there were free of charge, or very low rate busses that picked a girl up from her door step and dropped her right in front of school. Girls could most likely afford these busses, well because we were paid by the government to attend college. And if you were in a household with two or more children, note that here children are your children until they are capable of comfortably standing on their own feet which may happen somewhere in their mid-twenties and could afford to buy each a car then you could most likely afford one car and hire a driver who would cater to the whole family. The more fortunate was probably studying in Europe or the States and driving her own car. We went to school, the mall, our friend's houses and rarely if ever missed out on weddings or funerals. We got to where we wanted to be, who cares who was behind the wheel or what the car looked like."

"Still, wasn't there a time when you wished you could just get in a car and take off?"

She fell silent. I'm sure there must have been a time when she wished she didn't have to wait to drive a loved one to the emergency room, or make embarrassing phone calls to mothers from her son's class to bring her son home because her driver unexpectedly called in sick. Yes, we all had a moment when we wished we could drive. For me it was the day it took my father less than a minute to transform me from his princess to a free loading parasite. I had just carried both my kids upstairs after an hour of begging my sick Dadi to drink her soup and suddenly all I could think of were donuts. I asked my father if his driver who was on his way back could buy me and my son a donut. The store was just two minutes from my parent's house. "Why? Where's your driver?" he asked.

"He's back home, it will take him forty-five minutes to get here," I said.

"So? let him come and buy you donuts."

That was the moment I wished I could get in a car, buy donuts and keep driving until I reached a home where my desires weren't undermined. Forty-five minutes of holding my tears back and singing to my kids felt longer than a life time.

But we would never tell a stranger anything like that.

"What about having to wear the Abaya when you left

your house?"

"In every society a line is drawn in respect to general taste, right? In the freest of countries you still can't walk around a mall naked. If not arrested, you would be frowned upon and someone might yell at you, or even attack you. A line is a line regardless of where it is drawn, and we as a civilized people must have the decency to respect that line. I would wear my hijab wherever I was in the world and that is my choice."

She looked at us, I in my see-through colorful abaya, Hala in her jeans and black cardigan and asked, "If you were going somewhere else where you knew people would be more conservative you would cover your head, wouldn't you?"

"Yes, and I'm sure your friend only wears swimming shorts when he's going to the beach otherwise even on days when it's really hot he would wear a polo shirt and pants to work," Hala answered.

The lady giggled and introduced us to Alex, a cultural explorer and blogger.

"What about dating and arranged marriages? That must have been tough?" He looked straight at Hala.

"You know how best-selling western self-help books are all about the law of attraction. How you pay so much money to learn that you can manifest your perfect partner?"

"Yeah," he smiled.

"Well, we knew this since we were babies. The only difference is while you believe they will appear in a bar or at a friend's party, we believe we can manifest them right into our living rooms."

"Why do you think it took the Kingdom so long to open

its doors to tourists?" he asked me now.

"How long have you been here Alex?"

"A week."

"Have you been invited to a Saudi home?"

"Yes, a couple of times. A student I met on my flight here invited me to have dinner with him and his family and when I was down in Jazan the day before yesterday, my tour guide invited me for lunch."

"What was it like?"

"Uff there was so much food. The family here had a display of sea food enough for twenty people and it was only me and four of them. The tour guide had a whole lamb on a giant tray of rice prepared for just me and a friend. They were all too generous."

"Here's the thing Alex, Hala and I could have been raised in neighboring houses, our mothers could have been sisters and fathers cousins but every time I would go to her house I would have to adjust my clothes and tone to match and respect her household and that is how you would come to learn that no two houses in this kingdom follow the same rules, but one thing we will all have in common is how generously we welcome our guests. Now if I invite you over for coffee, I won't wait for you to ring the bell and ask you if you like your coffee with milk and sugar. I would have run down to my favorite pastry shop, placed the selection on my best China, filled a thermos with Saudi coffee, and offered you dates and then made you that black cup of coffee just the way you like. And if you come over for lunch or dinner there will be a welcoming juice, appetizers, side dishes and dessert. We would always make sure to fill your eyes before your stomach. Obviously when the Kingdom invited guests, it's hospitality could be nothing less than a spectacle and that takes time to prepare.

When you are invited to someone's kingdom, enjoy the generosity with which they welcome you, and the love with which they share their most intimate stories, don't go peeking behind closed doors, poking at wounds that may have not hurt before you poked, because in life what happened a minute ago doesn't matter."

Seduced

Bollywood movies with their alluring colors and captivating music seduced me into believing there was an end. A final resting place where people could just be. I watched a man travel across continents, social circles, caste, time and sometimes lives to find his woman. Their unexplainable collision stirred the world into a storm of confusion and everyone who knew the hero and heroine was dutifully deployed to restore order, their very few friends stood with them against an army of officials or thugs. Many heartbreaking tears and songs later, the opposing army, led by the girl's Father surrendered. He allowed his heart to be a heart and melt the grip of his hand. He let go of his crying and begging daughter's wrist. The girl ran to the arms of her love who up until that moment was so full of fury, he could have been beaten up by twenty men but still threatened to rip the stars out of the sky and place them at her feet. He hugged her, wiped her tears and all that fury vanished behind his closed eyes. The girl's Mother thanked the gods for sparing her daughter, finally a woman of her lineage was not expected to sacrifice every bit of herself to honor her family. The world rejoiced to a more relaxed song. There was no more hoping or trying, everything sat in place. Dadi and I took a deep breath, secretly wiped our own tears and a three hour emotional whirlpool came to an end.

My engagement to Essa and my childish love for

Abdullah shrunk down to a small corner of my mind. All I wanted now was a resting place where I could lay my head in the warmth of a shoulder. I wanted that bliss where everything else ended.

My grandmother must have had a hunch, for after every Bollywood movie we watched together she asked me, "Why can't you find someone at work?"

"Dadi, I go there to work not to hunt for grooms."

"Find someone," she would say, and I would laugh.

Work started at eight o'clock and since the first rule of selling your brand was subtle visibility. I was in the office by seven forty-five. That way I was well settled and seen by everyone who walked in after me.

I took two fifteen minute coffee breaks and spent them listening to whoever god sent my way. CEO, tea boy, accountant, IT manager, HR director, intern, Brand Manager or Sales Man. Because everyone knows something you don't and if you listen carefully enough, they tell you exactly what you need to hear. Office hours finished at five, I bought some lunch and headed down to one of our stores. We had six retail stores. I visited a different one every day because I needed to understand my two key players, my customer and my salesmen. I monitored them both and waited until the store closed at eleven to have a small discussion with my team. I socialized with family and friends only on Fridays while dedicating every other waking hour to my job. Four years later I was granted the title of Marketing Manager which earned me many business trips.

I picked a cup of coffee off the counter at a stall in Beirut and when I turned around, I almost bumped into a tall man who was standing too close behind me. I headed to a restaurant to meet my colleagues for lunch, he walked in a few minutes later, sat alone and stared right at me.

One of the girls, Tamara, was always so loud she annoyed the hell out of me. I made up a story in my mind about her to make it easier to tolerate her for the next two days. She lived in a house where no one listened to her when she spoke, so when she came out and someone listened, it wasn't enough. She needed the whole world to hear. "Sam, we're going to the movies at six tomorrow in Dunes. Would you like to join us?" she yelled to a man sitting two chairs away from her in a very quiet restaurant. I expected Saeed to come to the Cinema, I also turned around at the exact moment he walked into the theatre and sat down behind me. Ten minutes into the movie he cleared his throat and gently bumped my chair as he got up. I followed him out, he stopped right there by the door, took my phone out of my hand and dialed his number (No! passcodes did not exist back then). Without saying a word, he held the door open for me. I went back inside, and he was gone.

He called me late enough for me to be back at my hotel room. He lived in Jeddah too and was in Beirut on a short vacation. He changed his reservations so we could be on the same flight back home. Just on the same flight, we wouldn't dare sit together. A month later we were wishing each other a happy Eid. "What are you doing tomorrow?" he asked me.

"I'm going to have breakfast at The Hilton with my family and will probably come back and sleep. I only have three days off work. What about you?"

"I'm going to be at the Hilton watching you from a distance," he said.

"If you like him and think you want to marry him, don't go out with him," Raed warned me, so I came up with an excuse every time Saeed asked if we could meet. (Because back then boys rarely married a girl they went out with. They dated someone for as long as they wanted to but couldn't trust a girl that went out with them had not been out with someone else before them, and god forbid someone recognize their wife later. So they had their mothers find them a good girl preferably too young to have even known anything about the world and married her).

One day Saeed invited me to a forum where he was giving a speech. I went because it was a public place and it wasn't considered going out with him. I was seated at a row reserved for his guests along with his father and some friends. After a mesmerizing speech almost delivered just for me, he introduced me to his father as Marketing Manager of my company. Turns out Saeed and his dad were quite close and told each other everything. So a week later when his mother sat in our living room, she told my mother that her husband met me at a forum and instantly decided I was the perfect match for their son.

My mother requested some time to consult with my father and I used that time to call Saeed, "Your mother is here."

"Yes."

"Why didn't you say anything?"

"Because this is the proper way. You don't have to say anything to me, take your time and give your answer to your parents."

"But are you sure you want to marry me? You barely know me."

"I know what I need to know. I've seen how you behave amongst colleagues. I've seen how you behave abroad, what you're like with your family, your grownups and how you behaved with my father. What else do I need to know. Go now I will see you if your parents invite me for a formal meeting before we get engaged."

My mother came to my room and asked me if I was willing to meet the boy. I said yes and saw a spark in her eyes but she kept a straight face. I stuck my ear against the door to listen as she gave my future mother in-law the news. They both shied away from celebrating too soon. "Whatever Allah decides," they said to each other. Just as our guest was walking out the door my mother asked, "May I know what your son's last name is?"

Hasan, I whispered I had seen it on the banners at the forum.

"His full name is Saeed Hasan Alzahrani," the mother answered. I cursed myself, that was the same tribal last name my mother had a problem with. I braced myself and waited for her to tell me the wedding was off but instead, that weekend my parents sat in front of Saeed Alzahrani's family and all humility aside made ridiculous demands. My Meher was to be no less than thirty thousand Riyals and his family had to chip in on a big wedding, since I was the first child to get married in the family, they planned on inviting the whole city.

That was the night I called Raed and said goodbye.

As soon as I hung up, I received a phone call from my future mother in-law. She sweetly congratulated me and complimented my look from earlier that evening, then invited me to have lunch with them the next day.

Saeed had only seen me with straight hair, so I curled it for the occasion. I wore a wrap around floral dress and high heels. His mother received me at the door. "You're late!" she said in a sharp tone. You said lunch! I almost answered back.

"I'm sorry I was afraid you might not wake up early on a weekend and didn't want to disturb you," I said instead.

"Come, you can help me make Saeed's favorite dish." She took my Abaya and led me to the kitchen.

"Here, you chop the onions while I boil the meat." She pointed me toward a cutting board.

She was making lamb. I did not eat lamb. I couldn't handle the smell of it when it was served and here I was chopping onions and drowning in the smoke coming out of that boiling pot. "Oh no, that's too big. Layla! do you even know how to chop an onion?" she asked with that tone again.

"I don't cook," I shyly answered.

Three hours later, we served lunch. My father in-law stepped out of his office and Saeed came out of his bedroom stretching and yawning. "Surprise!" his mother yelled presenting me, with my stinky hair and sweaty forehead. I forced the food down my throat and waited for someone to compliment my cooking. At my parent's house we always complimented the chef. "This is the best lamb I've ever had Mama. Thank you for teaching me how to make it," I said to my mother in-law. She smiled with pride and when we were done cleaning the table, she allowed me to go freshen up in Saeed's bathroom. He came into the room, sat on his bed and told me he had to send out a few emails. I quietly fell asleep on an arm chair in the corner and when I woke up, Saeed was lying on his bed looking at me. I smiled and walked up to him.

"Are you done?" I asked.

He nodded his head and reached his hand out to me, I placed my hand in his, he kept his palm straight open, so I gently stroked it. He watched as my fingers moved from his wrist to the tip of his fingers, I watched him slowly melt away. "If I close my hand and catch you, I won't let you go," he mumbled then jumped to his feet and said, "Let's take you home." I thanked my in-laws for the beautiful day and left with him. He walked me up to my bedroom, followed me inside and closed the door. I panicked, what would my parents say. He reached his hand out again and I obediently gave him mine. This time he closed his hand and pulled me close into him. "I told you I wouldn't let you go," he whispered and kissed me.

"Wait, I have to tell you something."

"What?"

"I was engaged before."

"I know, your father told me." He kissed me.

"Not just that, I also knew other boys."

"I know, your mother told me." He kissed me.

"Shh, enough! you were lost and I saved you," he said as he kissed me.

Wait! Saved me, what?

I wanted to push him away but heard my aunts voice repeatedly threatening me. This is your second engagement, if you mess this up, you won't get another chance. You'll be alone forever.

I loved weddings and attended as many as I could. Sometimes I even went on behalf of my mother who wasn't so keen on celebrations and didn't mind. I always made it a point to dance to express my happiness for the bride on her special night. We owed her at least that much even if I was from the groom's side and did not know her or in some cases would never see her again, I still danced with joy. And by some miracle all that joy was returned to me at my wedding.

A few people my father knew from work assigned their daughters to plan me a week of Indian themed festivities. These girls I had never met before spent a whole day scrubbing my face and body with a golden paste, they applied Henna to my hands and feet and choreographed dances to be performed by my sister and cousins on the big Mehndi Night.

My father had the house decorated with flowers and lights. I watched him welcoming guests into his home with pride for the first time. He introduced them to four types of different bread that were being freshly made next to the fountain, told them which one went best with the Mutton and which with Daal. He explained the music and led people on the dance floor. He walked them through traditions and laughed loudly when they got something wrong. For the first time in ages he was not the outsider. My father was not ashamed of his broken Arabic accent, for this was an Indian/Pakistani celebration where he was not the minority.

He never blended into the Saudi society and always went back to Pakistan and India on alternating years to bond with family and friends on either side of the border. That night my father didn't have to answer the question, "Where are you from?" like he would at a vegetable stand, super market or restaurant when he chose to speak to the person serving him in Urdu/Hindi. When he was asked where he was from, I saw my father pause and answer Karachi if he believed the person was from Pakistan and if he believed that person was Indian, he would say Hyderabad. I grew up witnessing how nations and borders, a concept invented by man to bring people together, constantly left my father standing on the outer edge. On my Mehndi Night no one asked him where he was from, and he could comfortably be both Indian and Pakistani.

Then my aunts and my mother's childhood neighbors planned me a Saudi Ghumrah. They brought me a beautiful heavily embroidered beduin thobe, a gold belt and head piece. They covered me in a green veil and followed me out with soft drumming as the elder ladies hummed old folk songs.

And finally the extravagant wedding my mother had been planning since I was four. I walked down an Isle with Saeed. The floor was covered with red rose petals, and the stage we were headed toward decorated in a warm flowery hue. Behind the romantic song my cousins and I so carefully chose to link to my most precious memory, you could hear the women murmuring a soft prayer. I felt so blessed.

He hated being the only man in a giant hall packed with three hundred women watching his every step. He hated the photographer for giving him too many instructions. He told me to smile more, relax and engage with him in a conversation about how silly my whole wedding was "With all this money I could have bought you a beautiful dress and given you a nice wedding in Italy." But you did not pay for anything and what's wrong with my dress? I did not say. I took a deep breath and convinced myself he was just nervous.

We spent our honeymoon in Rome. A city where love dwells in the walls of ruins which may have witnessed many horrors but tell only the story of passion with which they were built. The hotel manager welcomed us like we were long lost family. Restaurant owners cooked their homemade pasta like a mother who was about to introduce her baby to his first meal. Violinists on the street, artists consumed in their canvases and newlyweds holding hands. Just being there was enough reason for me to fall in love with my husband.

We came back home. Saeed dropped me and the luggage off and went to see his friends. I walked through my one bedroom apartment like a queen strolling around her kingdom. I admired the paint, liked the dining table and planned to change the sofa. I reminded myself I had to do my own laundry now and figure out dinner, we both had work the next day. Just as I finished loading the washing machine, my mother's driver rang the bell with food. Dadi sent my favorite shrimp biryani. I waited for Saeed then called him a couple of times. "I'll be home soon," he told me around midnight. I lost my appetite and couldn't stay up any longer so I went to sleep. Saeed came home around three a.m. like he did every night from then on.

He came back from work at six every day ate the food I served him, slept on the sofa until it was dark then took a shower, splashed himself with perfume and went to see his friends. I would do some chores, send out a few emails and lie in bed staring at the ceiling. It was hard for me to sleep in the silence, after always having someone or the other talk me to sleep for so many years.

"My mom is picking me up in a bit, we're going to the mall," I told Saeed before he stepped out one evening.

"Why?" he asked.

Something cringed in my stomach as I answered, "We might do some shopping and have coffee."

"If you don't need anything urgent I can take you tomorrow. Why would you go to the mall at night?" he said to me that once and since then I never went to the mall after sunset.

"Sure." I said. He went out and I spent another evening alone.

"Where are all your friends' wives? When they spend the whole night out with you?" I eventually asked.

"They have their own gatherings with their girl friends or family."

"Every night?"

"I don't know."

"What do you guys do?"

"We just hang out; some play cards others watch a game. Nothing special."

"Why are you married if you don't want to spend time with your wives?"

"I knew you wanted to pick a fight." He lost his temper.

"I'm not picking a fight, I'm just wondering what you expect me to do when you're out every day."

"Why don't you go see your friends?"

"You'd be okay with that? Me being out until three in the morning?" I became a little louder.

"No, you don't have to stay until three, I can pick you up earlier."

"Well I don't want to go out with my friends every night. I married you so I could spend time with you!" I couldn't control my frustration and started to cry. He saw my tears, opened his cabinet, stuffed some clothes into a backpack and left.

At four a.m. I sent him a message apologizing and blaming my outrage on hormones from my contraceptives. He came home a few minutes later and we pretended that argument never happened.

A big work event was coming up in Dubai which consumed most of my attention leaving me no time to worry about Saeed's whereabouts.

I'll be late at work today, I have a conference call at seven, I texted him one afternoon.

At seven fifteen I received a text from him saying, *I'm waiting for you at the reception.* I met him there two hours later. "Who else is in the office?" he asked me.

"No one! Would you like to come in?"

"Yes, I need to use the bathroom." He scanned the place and asked me, "Why, couldn't you make this phone call at home?"

"I had a lot of other work to do."

"Look how dark it is, there is no one in the building. How can your bosses leave you here alone?" I was confused, did he want someone to be there with me? Or was he relieved I was alone?

"It's my job, Saeed. They don't care that I'm a woman."

"Well they should."

"I'm sorry I won't let anything like this happen again, okay?" I was too tired to argue.

"Okay." He sounded like my mother.

Saeed showed up at my office more often, he introduced himself to my bosses, pointed out flaws in my proposed strategies and offered them free consultation. They loved him and I hated that he was invading my space. He called me around lunch hour to make sure I was still in the building and one day he swore he saw me leave with someone. Between work, maintaining a clean house and entertaining his silly mind games I was exhausted, and finally a day before my flight to Dubai, I allowed the question that was stuck in my throat for weeks to come out. "Do you want me to quit my job?"

"I can't ask you to quit your job but I would be happier if you did. I promise I will give you double your salary, just stay home. It is my responsibility to provide for you."

I did not go to Dubai, work to me was never about money. Only that first Dolce and Gabbana bag and Armani dress meant something after that, they were just bags, shoes and clothes. I never had to pay rent or bills so quitting my job was just quitting on expensive things I could survive without. Only I wasn't quitting my job, I was quitting my passion. I was leaving that road I solemnly walked leading toward myself and falling into a cart wagon pulled by my husband in whichever direction he pleases.

Favors and sacrifices are two very different things. With favors you have leverage, a string you can tug on to bring things back to order. But when you sacrifice a horse, a soldier an army or your crown for the greater peace of your kingdom there is no guarantee to how long that peace would last.

With every ring on the phone, my heart said this is it. This is the one where he says be ready I'm picking you up in an hour, I made reservations. With every cluck of the door my heart said this is it, this is the one where he kisses your eyes for waiting up, this is the one where he kisses your hand for making his favorite lamb.

I tried to break the cycle and planned date nights. Saeed would pick me up from home late enough for us to have to change our reservations but not bother coming out of the car to change his clothes. On our way to a restaurant, he would either be on the phone or road rage. He would find something wrong with the food or the table or how long it took us to be served. We would rush through dinner so he could drop me back home and catch up with his friends and when he came back, he always found it easier to criticize me than compliment me.

"Hala is getting engaged and she wants me to go with her to the Beauty Salon," I told him one day before he left for work. What remained of my last paycheck was running out and I needed money. I knew Saeed couldn't afford to double my salary back then and made do with whatever he gave me.

"She's getting married?" He failed to hide his sarcasm.

"Yes."

"Poor guy, May Allah help him."

"Anyway, I can go right?"

"You're only going to the Beauty Salon? If you go anywhere else let me know," he said as he handed me some cash.

"Okay."

Hala and I sat next to each other at the nail station, our feet soaking in a warm lather and finger nails being painted in dark red.

I tried real hard to stop myself but ended up asking, "Hala, are you sure about this guy? Have you met him?"

"Yes, I told you they came over on Sunday."

"I mean after that? Or before that? One meeting in your living room with your parents watching can't be enough for you to decide you want to marry him. I always thought you of all people would want to marry for love."

"Ah! Well I learnt from your parents that love is overrated, an emotion constructed by humans for god knows what purpose."

"What?"

"If love were all it was made out to be, don't you think you and Abdullah would have ended up together? The whole universe attested to your love. Do you think it was a coincidence that his eyes somehow pierced through space and found you wherever you went in this big city? Then what? A word from your mother was enough for you to leave him. I hope she's happy now that you're married to Saeed Alzahrani's shadow. I can learn to love Ahmed; he seems nice enough."

"But you know what they say about pilots!" (Back in the day they said pilots were not trustworthy. All that traveling, they were exposed to more foreign women than anyone and most likely tempted to take second wives).

"That's nonsense! His father is a pilot and still married to just his mother. My mom asked," she giggled, then added, "what other choice do I have? You've seen the guys I meet."

"We don't step into a shit hole just because all the other routes are stinky Hala!"

"Why not?"

"Because you never know how deep that pile of shit is!"

"I'm almost thirty if I want to have kids now is the time, I can't wait for someone who may never show up." Back then we were also led to believe it was impossible to have kids when you were passed thirty-five.

"You're going to be the most beautiful bride," I told her with a smile and she was.

Hala became a wife molded from romantic tales and ever after. She wore colorful dresses, slippers with tiny heals and always smelt like expensive perfume and freshly baked cake. She welcomed Ahmed home with a candle light feast, offered him pedicures and lay out fresh pajamas for him on the bed. She wrapped him in a delicate slumber and woke him to mornings worthy of kings. Between flights, Ahmed buried himself in sleep and presented Hala with a stinky slob for a husband.

She tried everything she could to bring out the prince of her dreams she so strongly believed was hiding somewhere inside him. She spent thousands on books written by promising marriage experts and watched hundreds of how to make your man fall in love with you videos. Dragging her heavy corpse like husband behind her, she followed every advice to resuscitate her marriage. They did family gatherings and dinners. She tried to manipulate him like a child and requested him like an adult. She sent out hints in songs and wrote him straightforward letters. "Call me sometimes just to say you missed me, walk toward me when you come home and take a minute to kiss me," she begged him. She decorated her walls with beautiful portraits of herself and snooped through his phone. Ahmed wasn't seeing anyone else he just failed to see that Hala belonged to a different realm and over romanticized everything, just a little bit from him would have gone a long way.

Ahmed learnt all about marriage from his parents. The man goes out to make money, comes home to a house full of respect and a meal served by the woman. The kids kiss his hands and disappear into their rooms giving him quiet time alone while his wife cleans up. Romance was nothing but a sinful act displayed in movies he was never allowed to watch at home.

Noise

Saeed and I spent two years trying to get pregnant. I locked myself in the bathroom for hours every time I spotted my period then wiped my tears and begged Allah to forgive me for hurting my mother's feelings. "If this is how you choose to punish me so be it," I said to him. I'd rather be punished here on earth than rot in hell for all eternity.

Saeed saw my swollen eyes and planned a trip to the Hogwarts of Happiness, Cairo. The common man will teach you that unlike everything you knew about happiness it is not this far away goal you have to pursue. It is a simple phrase (Idhak hua had wakhed minha haga) Laugh, no matter how bad it gets for one day we leave it all behind.

The sound of his laughter washed out the noise of his choked up misery. The sound of my laughter washed out the noise of my guilt. The sound of Saeed's laughter washed out all the hurt he caused me. And all was good, because simply it was nothing but noise we allowed to linger in our heads.

I had never been to Cairo and found the accent a little challenging. Saeed worried about me being tricked into paying too much attention or money to the Egyptian so he never let go of my hand. I allowed him to lead me through alleys, restaurants and dance floors. The less composed I was, the more my husband embraced me. I watched him introduce food, shake to music and so passionately explain the culture to me.

When we came back, I unpacked our luggage and realized how the sanitary pads occupying half my suitcase had not been touched. I kept quiet for another two weeks.

I did not want to tell Saeed anything until I was sure. So I asked my mother to take me to the hospital. I also believed that maybe if she saw how badly I wanted a baby she would allow Allah to forgive me. The doctor showed me something on the ultrasound screen and confirmed a healthy pregnancy. I hugged my mother tightly, kissed her hands and pressed them against my eyes. She spread out a small prayer rug in the hospital corridor and told me to join her for a prayer. "May Allah always bless you with health and happiness. I stayed up every night praying for this," she tearfully uttered as she kissed my forehead.

I rushed home, made dinner and gave Saeed the news.

A tiny being pushed out of my body and my soul resided somewhere under his flaky skin. A blink later he let out a giggle that captivated my heart like a Sufi Hymn.

When Oday almost turned two, Allah blessed me with another pregnancy. I wasn't surprised to receive Saeed's message that he would not be making it to the ultrasound appointment again. Still, I wished he could be there, it was the one where the doctor promised to reveal the gender.

I called him as I got back into the car.

"How did it go? Is everything okay?" he asked.

"Yes."

"I just closed a Four Million Riyal deal. Your husband is a genius, you should have seen me in that meeting room."

"That's great! I'm so proud of you."

"I have to go now, will see you at home later."

"Okay, bye." I hung up without telling him what the doctor said.

I can't explain but after Saeed, Dada was the first person I wanted to tell I was pregnant with a girl. Old age struck him down, he could barely move on his own anymore and spent most of his day on a recliner watching TV. I placed Oday on his lap and sat on the floor next to him making sure my son did not hurt him and that he did not drop my son.

"Dada, how come you never trusted me to handle your company?" I asked him.

"Who said I didn't trust you?"

"Well you did, you always made it clear that my brother would handle the business, you made sure he studied well and got good grades and always pointed out that I needed a husband."

"Do you need money? You know all of this is yours, how much do you need? I'll call the accountant right now."

"Not Money, I need passion."

"You're passionate about a construction office?" he asked with a sarcastic chuckle.

"No, but I could find passion in keeping my grandfather's dream alive!"

"The company was never my dream," he said, this time a little more seriously.

"Then what was?"

"This!" He waved his hands around gesturing to the house.

"I'm an Architect, I wanted to build a beautiful house. The office helped make enough money to do so. And you know what brought it to life?"

"What?" I asked

"The noise you and your siblings made" He smiled.

"It's a girl this time." I placed his hand on my belly.

"Thank god." He teared a little and kissed my hand.

"When she asks you what you are passionate about, you tell her you are passionate about the only thing worth being passionate about, life.

You tell her, her mother was always passionate about life. She always wanted to try everything new, phone booths, double decker busses and ferries. She wildly danced to loud music behind a closed door. That same door hugged her when she screamed in defeat. She excelled in school and easily climbed up the business ladder. She fell in love with one and conquered the hearts of many. She is the most feminine of women, she is also a boy's best friend and a man's backbone." I smiled wondering how much more he knew about me. "That's right, I hear and see everything and from where I'm looking you have everything you need to pursue your passion," he added.

He called me back when I reached the end of the hallway, "Layla!"

"Yes Dada."

"Are you going upstairs?"

"Yes."

"Tell Dadi I'm sorry." I was about to ask, what for? For everything he had ever done, or did he do something again? But the look in his eyes answered my question.

Dada suffered a couple of strokes that left him bed ridden and in clear pain. He, a man true to his principle, refused to die and leave his wife without a guardian. For as long as he was alive, he was feared and no one dared to disturb Dadi's peace.

A few years later, she was diagnosed with cancer and at her second admission to the hospital, she waited for everyone to be present, looked my father straight in the eye and said "No more hospitals, take me home."

Those were her last words. After which, she shut her mouth with all the little might she had left in her and starved herself to death. Shortly after my grandfather relieved from all responsibility, allowed himself to go.

With them gone, my father and aunts scratched at each other's throats. They all wanted the house, but no one wanted to sit at the head of the table. No one wanted to take the kids on evening walks or make sure everyone had their favorite dish for lunch. No one cared to fix the damage or contain the damaged.

It takes a village to raise a child, no the internet can't compensate for a village. The internet is like a judgmental mother in-law, never lends you a hand but constantly tells you where you're falling short. When my mother's mother felt her first attack of nausea the whole neighborhood celebrated. Her mother, sisters and aunts took turns cleaning and cooking for her. Not that they needed to cook, a young boy knocked at their door every few hours with half of what his mother was serving them for breakfast, lunch and dinner. Someone stitched clothes for the baby, someone helped her deliver the baby under the stairs and someone breastfed the infant so she could get an extra hour of sleep. By the time my grandmother had her third child she and her neighbor Fatima were inseparable. Tired of their shenanigans, their husbands decided to bolt the doors from outside when they left for work. My grandmother and

Fatima used their kitchen tools to dig a hole through the wall between them. They crawled through, cleaned, cooked, sang, danced, rolled cigarettes and smoked together. They took turns feeding the children out of pots and their breasts. The kids grew up between both mothers and all their other neighbors. There was always an eye watching them and always a hand feeding them. Sweaty and barefoot, they gathered around an elder who told them stories about Prophets and Caliphs. Another rewarded them with candy for praying at the mosque. The man selling frozen fruit water off a trolly would accept the fifty cents a girl waved at his face and give all the kids a pack each. My grandmother became Ummi (mother) to her children and all the men and women who grew up in that neighborhood. She became Ummi to all their children and grandchildren. To the doctors, teachers, vendors, drivers, mechanics and plumbers. We all marched around her, making sure she was never disappointed. Because somehow we all shared a belief that if her heart were ever touched by sadness a horrible wrath was sure to be unleashed upon us.

Nowadays, if you are lucky, your mother would come spend a month with you post-delivery. Aunts, cousins and friends would visit you to judge how much you spent on decorating the hospital room. You live in an expensive neighborhood and warn your kids from being too loud. You don't allow them to step outside the house because it is unsafe. Your kids rush in and out of a mosque only if their fathers were free to take them and even when it is your own parents handing them candy, they look at you for approval.

My children's grandparents were too busy following their careers, physically and mentally exhausting themselves trying to prove that they were smarter than people half their age. Well, if not that then what? We made it clear we would rather live in small apartments than with them. Our children were too busy staring at screens to chase my father out for a walk, they did not know what night terrors were and their bed time routine left no room for my mother to sleep with them.

My brother was somewhere following his dream and my sister was studying in the states, alone, and when she came back, she was too sophisticated to be a simple aunt. One evening after she was back, she and my mother sat with me on the dining table as I fed Oday spoonful's of rice and his baby sister dug her head in my arm pit trying to sleep. My baby sister was busy texting with a devious smile on her face, then she excused herself, went to her bedroom and closed the door. I held my kids closer to my body and waited for my mother to grab her cloak and initiate her exorcism ritual. Instead she gave me a broken smile and recited a new verse "times have changed."

"Time can't change, Mama, it is nothing but a tool we invented to brag about our progress. People change, and they choose when. Or sometimes they don't have much of a choice." I smiled back at her.

My poor mother was a middle child of an evolving kingdom, stuck in the wake of change. Half of her submerged in a sea of beliefs while the other half was being splashed by a new norm every day. I was her child, if she had not held on tight enough she would have lost me to darkness. My sister was also her child, if she held on to her with a hint of tightness she would have lost her to that same darkness, only that's not what it's called anymore.

Nowadays they call it socializing with people of their generation.

So what if my kids did not have a village. Two of the strongest humans set aside all their small battles, all their unfulfilled desires, hopes and dreams and took an oath. They would do anything so their children could have everything. Saeed took off like a storm. The world tried to stumble him, stabbed him in the back and tried to pull him down but he kept rising. He seized every opportunity and conquered. I promised to hold down the fort and keep every distraction inside so he could charge on without looking back. I changed diapers, cooked and cleaned. I got used to eating every meal alone. I grew used to my husband being gone for days. It was okay, I was a warrior princess strong enough to handle it. Saeed grew bigger, he built an empire, we hired a maid, driver and gardener to serve us. I was a queen trusted with the most sacred gems the world had come to know, my children. I marched them to school, gyms and playgrounds, staring everyone in the eye, threatening them, "If anyone so much as disturbed my children's peace, I will summon all the rage god invested in every mother's womb and unleash upon the world."

Saeed grew bigger, he reminded me that he and he alone built this empire. I could not afford to change a sofa; it was beyond the money I had in hand. I could not choose a paint color or buy a mug, not a day went by without him questioning my every decision. "Why did you buy that? Why did you cook chicken and not meat? Why did you put that there?" I was degraded to supervisor of staff by day, whose job was to make sure everything sat exactly where he and his kids liked, the fridge was stacked and food was served on demand. By evening I was a mistress who had to entertain the emperor's every thought, if I wanted to continue to live in that house with my kids. Because a wife degraded to supervisor of staff was easier to replace than a well-trained maid, all it took was the word I divorce you repeated three times and puff she disappeared. At least a maid had a contract and an end of service disclaimer. All a wife had was the dignity to call her father to pick her up.

I went to sleep and when I woke up my children had outgrown me. I ran out of things to teach them, and they taught me bigger lessons.

Oday taught me that you didn't really need to create noise in your head to wash out noise. Sometimes all you needed was silence to help you see. He barged out of his room in tears, his face red and sweaty. "What happened?" I panicked and searched his body, his father jumped to his feet and yelled at him to speak.

"Saif ruined my Island. I was building it my whole life." He was playing online with his best friend Saif. He was nine and had been working on that virtual Island for months. He spent all his allowance and playtime building it.

Which to him was his whole life. I felt sorry for him and told him he did not have to be friends with Saif anymore. He could easily make new friends who respected his boundaries and efforts. His father told him to be a man. "Go break his Island!" he said. Saif's mother called and apologized on her son's behalf. She promised to punish him whichever way Oday found appropriate. My son ran to his room and closed the door. I followed him in. "Are you okay?" I asked.

"I need you all to be quiet, you're making too much noise," he said.

"Okay." I walked out and told everyone to leave him alone.

He came out and watched TV with us for a while then his iPad rang. It was Saif. "Hello Oday, do you want to play?" he said.

"Yes, but a different game."

Oday and Saif are still best of friends, but they never played that game again and always refrain from playing games that could tempt them to upset each other.

Then he turned eleven and became less like me and more like his father until one day he even asked me the dreadful, Why? I hated that now he too questioned my every decision and although I was willing to let it slide with his father, when Oday asked me why we dropped his sister to school first, why was I reading a whole book on my phone or why I had to change his bedsheets on Wednesday, I felt like slapping him but figured a better way to stop him would be to answer his every sarcastic question until he got tired of asking.

So when he asked me again, why we dropped his sister to school first? I said, "Because she loves being early and you complained about having to wait fifteen minutes for first period."

"Oh okay, but you don't need to make a U-turn all the way back to the boy's gate, I can walk. I don't want you to get tired. Mama, I love you," he said.

I purposefully read on my phone in front of him and he asked again, "Why do you read books on your phone?"

"It's easier for me to buy them online," I said.

"You can use my iPad Mama, it's better for your eyes," he said. I hugged and thanked him and he told me he loved me.

He asked why we changed bedsheets on Wednesday when we did general cleaning on Saturdays just because he wanted to know.

Apparently Saeed wasn't questioning my decisions either, he just wanted to know how he could make things better. Did I not like the mugs he chose or need more money to buy a set. Did we run out of meat? did he need to call the butcher to order more. He wanted to know if I wanted him to help me rearrange bigger furniture and he wanted to spare me and my mother the inconvenience of going to a crowded mall and was just offering to buy me whatever I needed.

When I silenced the noises in my head, I saw that the true reason my stomach clinched at the sound of the word *Why?* Was because all my life in school and at home I was taught to never ask *Why?* Because *Why,* led to a bigger taboo, *What If?* And *What If?* allowed Satan to play with your mind and question the way things were supposed to be.

I remember the day I saw my daughter for the first time. A bundle of light. The nurse gently carried on open palms like she was afraid to smudge. They placed her head next to mine and she smiled you begged god for a child, he gave you two. We named her Maryam.

Maryam, proved to me that all women are mothers, they don't have to carry a child inside them to be so. You are a mother when you check on your brother for having a fever. When you humor him and laugh at his stupid jokes. You are a mother when you fight for your sibling's right to things you never had. You are a mother when you kiss your mother's tired eyes and call it giving her energies. You're a mother when you listen to your father repeatedly telling you the same story over and over again. You are a mother when you make the biggest sacrifices seem like nothing so your husband can have peace of mind. You're a mother when you pick that cat off the street. You're a mother when you love that dog to death. Sure men do these things too, but only a woman can do it tirelessly. Heaven lies under her feet who ever she is and whenever she is motherly.

Maryam is my village. She invites me to sing and dance. She invites me to walk bare foot on the sand and swim in the ocean. She allows me to overreact and forgivingly welcomes me back. She encourages me to do handstands and claps for me even when I fail. She tells me I'm beautiful sometimes in words, others by just being the breathtaking creature that she is. Everyone who meets her tells me to never change her personality. May Allah help me not to. I pray that I'm blessed to be there for as long as she needs me. I pray that I have the strength to control my fears and watch her fly. I pray I have the courage to share the beauty of my beliefs without forcing them on her. I pray that I have the wisdom to see beyond her fake smiles and open the door when she cries.

Maryam's glowing receptive eyes teach me to believe in the abundance of Allah' s riches and that it's okay to want all that life has to offer you.

If It is Freedom You Seek You Must First Identify/ The Chains You Are Shackled To

Along came a tall and handsome prince. He did not save one Cinderella but all Cinderellas. He found their glass slippers but also brought them a new pair of running shoes. He slayed the dragon and all dogmas vanished. He left the door wide open for her to run out on her own.

I wasn't a Cinderella, I was her stepsister. Not the cunning one who imposed as Cinderella and married a prince. The gullible one who settled for the baker. Now I was forty-one at the peak of my physical health and beauty and because I had no magic wand to turn back time there was only one way for me to go from here, age gracefully. While I did that, my baker now no less than an emperor was surrounded by all sorts of women.

There were the young who grew up in conservative homes. The one thing these girls knew better than anyone else was beauty. Once reserved only for the eyes of their husbands they now flaunted their long dark hair across town. They wore full make up and high heels in broad day light. Because up until then the only outing they knew were all women parties. They only knew how to speak in one tone and had no filters. Like children who had been let out after being locked up in their playrooms, nothing was off limits.

There were the middle aged who jumped right off the

wagon and got divorced. For they too wanted to enjoy the perks of this new life, and life was too short to stay shackled to their dull, draining husbands. They did not wish to remarry, but that did not stop them from poking at men. All their lives they were told that a man would lose his mind if they went out with an uncovered face. So when they did reveal their surgically youthful faces and men did not lose their minds, it drove them crazy.

Then there was the next generation who knew exactly what running shoes were made for. They were exposed to enough of the world through travel, the internet and movies. They put their princess slippers away when they were seven and pulled them out occasionally. They understood well that there was a right time and place for everything. Their principles, modesty and faith stood strong giving merit to what the prince had come for.

Hala had two boys, around the same age as my children. When her youngest started to walk, she decided she wanted to go back to work. Ahmed did not want her to work with men. "Divorce me," she said. He was willing to allow it if she covered her face. "Divorce me," she said. He was willing to allow it if she did not wear make-up. "Divorce me," she said, packed her stuff, left her kids with the nannies and went to her mother's house.

"Why are you doing this Hala? You don't need a job and your kids are really young." I tried to talk some sense into her.

"Remember when we moved into this house?" she asked me.

"Yes."

"I was pregnant. Power and water lines weren't connected in the area yet. I had to go to the industrial district and haggle over a generator. Do you know how many women were there?"

"No."

"None! a whole district with no women. Then I went to the water truck stop and stood in line also among a hundred men for a whole hour. Ahmed was on a forty-five minute flight. He didn't call me until the next day. He didn't ask me if I was okay, if someone bothered me, if my head and face were covered or if I had any make up on. So what's he going on about now?

The boys will grow up soon and have their own lives, but no one will hire me when I'm older."

He caved, he had to. She was strong and he had two little children he could not possibly raise on his own. Over the years Hala tried to convince me to go with her to the other side of town to buy groceries at half price. Then she tried to convince me to buy cheaper clothes for myself and less toys for the kids. She no longer wore pretty dresses or proper perfume. "Ahmed doesn't deserve me to dress up for him," she said. She had her kids skip UN day at school because she believed it was ridiculous for her to buy them costumes they were only going to wear once. She always celebrated their birthdays at home and hand-crafted terrible decorations with a homemade cake. While I took my kids to amusement parks and spent hundreds, she only took her kids to public parks and bought them candy off street vendors. "Hala, your economic intelligence is slipping into cheap stinginess. I know you can afford better for the kids you just told me last week that you fought with Ahmed to increase your grocery money which was already a bit much for groceries, plus you have your own salary now. What are you doing with all the money?" I couldn't help but ask her after watching her refuse to buy her boys a toy despite all the heart melting begging. She brushed me off saying I was silly spending so much on things that were of no importance.

One day a news app bleeped an alert on my phone. A Saudi airplane almost crashed near the airport due to a malfunction, Ahmed was the pilot. I put on my abaya and rushed to Hala's office. The tea boy pointed me in the direction of a meeting room where she was hysterically tapping on her phone. "Hala, calm down. He's okay, I'm sure he'll call you in a bit." I held her tight, when I looked back up, we were surrounded by her colleagues. Some said they had just returned from the mosque where they prayed a gratification prayer, thanking Allah for her husband's well-being while others collected a donation and distributed the money to poor workers on the street to protect her and her family from bad events. The tea boy brought her a cup of warm milk to start a white page leaving behind any bad karma. I took my friend home and stayed with her until midnight. She barely ate and did not put her phone down for a second.

When we heard Ahmed's car pull in, I begged her not to fight with him. "Where were you?" she asked.

"I had to go see my mother. She was really shaken," he explained while looking at me.

"I was scared too. Thank god you're okay." She kissed his chest because that is where she reached, fell back on the sofa and finally cried. I was about to walk out, I looked back and saw Ahmed standing a meter and a half away from her with a smirk on his face and saying, "It is part of our job we are trained to expect to come face to face with a situation like this at least once in our career. That once we either survive or die. Don't make such a big deal out of this."

"Hold your wife, Ahmed! She slipped from a hundred thrones and fell on your sofa you lucky fool. Hold her before the heavens question god for writing her in your name," I said to him before I slammed the door. She had slipped from a hundred thrones, so many men chased her, I saw how desperately they wished the smile on her face was meant for them and here she was just a few steps away from a man she would have never looked at, crying, begging for him to hold her. I wished I could punch that smirk off his face.

Almost a year later, I ran into her at the kid's school. "Layla, can you come somewhere with me?" she asked.

"Sure, should we take your car or mine?"

"Yours, I don't want my driver to see where I'm going."

"Hala, please don't get me in trouble with Saeed."

"I won't, I promise."

I texted Saeed that I was going out for breakfast and we got into my car. She led me to an apartment in a building near her house. "What do you think?"

"It's nice, very well-lit and spacious. Who is it for?" I asked.

"I made a down payment yesterday, and my installment loan from the bank was approved. I won't be able to furnish it right away. Maybe if Ahmed lets me take my bedroom, otherwise I'll just bring the sofa from the boy's room. He won't notice it's gone. For now, I'm just going to make sure the kitchen is ready."

"I thought things were better between you and Ahmed. Didn't you say he works much less and started to spend time with you and the kids? He even makes lunch on Fridays, takes you out on Saturdays? You take more trips together?"

"Remember that day he came home after almost crashing?" She let out a heavy sigh.

"How could I forget?" She sat on the cold white marble floor of that empty apartment and talked to me after a very long time.

"When you left, he sat next to me and put his hand on my knee. I apologized for all the times I nagged about stupid things after he came back from work. I understand now how stressful your job could be, being responsible for so many lives, how scary those hours may be for you. Go get some rest I promise I will no longer ask you to do anything around the house please forgive me for being so insensitive. I said to him. He went to sleep without saying anything back. I stayed up all night thinking of what responsibilities I could take off his hands. You know what I figured out?"

"What?" I asked although I knew the answer.

"I was already doing everything alone. I registered the boys in school, attended parent meetings took them to hospital appointments, soccer practice, disciplined and spoiled, celebrated and broke down alone." She forgot to mention dealing with electricians, plumbers, running to the pharmacy in the middle of the night while Ahmed slept. She forgot to mention all that, but I knew.

"Hala they're all like that. You think Saeed helps with any of those things?"

"No, I know he doesn't. But let me ask you this?" she said. "What is your favorite moment of the day?"

"The look on my children's faces when I pick them up from school," I answered without a moment's hesitation.

"You know what the highlight of my day has been for ten years?"

"What?"

"When I see that Ahmed is online on some social media platform and I'm relieved he is alive. I never know where he is and have no one to call to make sure he is okay. Ever since we got married, I had been training to come face to face with a malfunction and holding my breath to see if our marriage survives.

I had a panic attack the next time he went to work after that flight. He told me he was flying to New York, I woke up in the middle of the night and couldn't breathe. I tried calling him, my calls and messages didn't go through. I called the airline and asked about his flight. We don't fly to New York today the man answered. I asked if Ahmed was scheduled on any flights, I can't give you that kind of information he chuckled. I cried and begged, he disappeared for fifteen minutes then transferred me to his supervisor who wanted to confirm I was his wife before he told me that Ahmed was on a flight to Paris."

"What did you do when he came back?"

"He came back four days later, I didn't say anything to him. I spent years waiting for him Layla, to be a prince, a husband, a father, a partner, a responsible roommate even. I got nothing.

Now, he decides it is time for him to call me before he boards a flight and as soon as he lands, he decides to play house and what? I'm supposed to pick up torn pieces of myself from all corners of that house and hand him a patched up me? He didn't even apologize.

This one responsibility I failed to take off his hands no matter how hard I tried, how am I supposed to apologize to myself on his behalf?

You see unlike you, my kids are not the center of my Universe. They are a beautiful gift from Allah I will always cherish. I am the center of my Universe and living with Ahmed deprives of my essence, he deprives me of my ability to charm leaving behind an angry cripple and all that negativity taints the joy I want to share with my kids."

"Does he hit you?" her parents asked.

"No."

"Then why do you want a divorce?"

Her parents couldn't understand why she was leaving such a perfect man and refused to help her unless she moved back into their house. "How will I and my two kids sleep in my old bedroom and share a bathroom with my sister?" she asked a question no one answered. She knew very well her parents were trying to suffocate her into going back to her husband because until a day before yesterday, a woman was only known to live in one of two houses, her parent's or her husband's. There was no such thing as a family supporting a woman to live on her own. Today girls from all over the Kingdom leave home and go to different cities to study or work, rent apartments and live on their own because times have changed but my friend remains frowned upon.

The next time I visited Hala in her apartment, she so proudly showed me the boy's room painted in dramatic blue, decorated with Super Hero wall art and the latest toys neatly displayed on shelves. She bought them queen size beds and covered them with beautiful blankets. "I just finished cleaning," she said as she fluffed the pillows.

"I can tell it smells so fresh."

"Do you think they'll like it?"

"Are you kidding me? They'll love it. When are they coming over?" I excitedly asked.

"Next weekend, their grandmother threw another party she wants them to attend this Friday. And I wasn't sure I could get rid of the paint smell in time so I did not make a big deal out of it. Next week is better, I'll be paid by then and can take them out for a nice dinner too."

Aside from that perfect boy's room the only other furniture in the apartment was the old sofa she managed to sneak out of her ex-husband's house which was also her bed and a used television one of her cousins gave her. I knew my friend only swallowed her pride and accepted the TV so her kids could play their video games.

At least Hala did not go through a long and painful custody battle. Her husband and in-laws only kept the boys long enough to poison their minds against her before they packed them up and dropped them at her doorstep.

Her boys complained about the food, blamed her for not loving their father enough or being as patient as a mother should be. She caught her elder nudging at his little brother if he smiled at her for too long or asked to sleep or cuddle with her. Every attempt to do school work always ended in a scream behind banged doors.

I literally had to drag Hala to our next teacher/parent conference. She was too embarrassed to face the teachers and I was too shy to go to the all boy school by myself because Saeed was too important to tend to such matters. Up until that year the boys were young enough to be in the girl's campus and I met their female teachers on a daily basis. This year they were all grown up and I had just a few chances when we were welcome to have an audience with the men who I trusted with my son for half the day. The teachers sat behind desks spread out across a spacious hall and parents lined up for a ten minute meeting with each. Turns out I had nothing to worry about, I was surrounded by Moms. There were a few Dads, some ridiculed their wives for making them take a day off. Some stared straight into our eyes and ridiculed our choice of men and others buried their chins in their chests offended by our invasion of their space.

Hala sat with the Science teacher first, then I took her place and she moved on to the English teacher. In the middle of my meeting with Oday's Math teacher, I heard my friend weep. I pulled her off the chair in front of Ustaadh Youssef, our kids' Arabic teacher and we rushed out through all the tongue clucking, and angry (Astaghfur Allah)s asking Allah to forgive us.

"What happened?" I asked her.

"He wrote nothing on his exam papers, not even his name."

"It's okay I'm sure if you talk to the principle they will allow him another chance. I can help you teach him, and he can retake the exam."

"That's not why I cried," she said as she wiped her tears.

"Why then?"

"Ustaadh Youssef said…" she sobbed again.

"What did he say?" I hugged her and asked.

"He said, you know I am here to help. He is my son too; all my students are. And on no Universe are you alone responsible for him. Just tell me what I can do."

Ustaadh Youssef a glorious personification of the Arabic language was a theatrical delight not only for the eyes of his students but for us parents too. He walked and dressed like a reincarnation of an Abbasid Emir. His cloak and turban, big smile and eyes lined with black kohl grabbed everyone's attention and since he believed he was from a different Era oblivious to current social laws, he stood in front of the school entrance and called upon Hala with his deep loud voice. "Oh Mother of my beloved student, may I request a minute of your time."

"What are you doing? Everyone is looking!" she snapped at him.

"What kind of a man do you take me to be. Brave enough to sadden your heart in front of everyone but too ashamed to mend it? Forgive me for failing you." He apologetically placed his hand on his heart and bowed his head.

"How have you failed me? I failed my son."

"He came to class and sat down for the Exam under my watch, if anyone failed him it was me. Again, please forgive me I promise I will make it up to you and him."

Hala cried again. "I'm sorry, I don't know why I'm crying. You must think I'm so weak. I will go now and maybe speak with you later. Thank you."

We left and a few days later when he saw her at the parking lot, he shouted, "Imagine we lived in a world full of strong trees and no fragile flowers. Where's the beauty in that?" Luckily, she was the only one who understood what he was talking about.

Ustaadh Youssef did not stop at that. He was after all a Beduin, brave not only on the battle field but also in his Ghazal.

He stuck a handwritten letter on the window of her car saying, *The day you pulled back your wild curls in a tight bun left me lost and scattered in thin air, like a gypsy's forgotten song.*

I beg you doom me to my fate, decide me one of two men

Your humble servant who will sit by your feet drumming his hands away while you dance

Or the love in who's arms all your storms come to an end

Hala avoided him for years, until her boys were no longer students of that school and old enough not to care about their mother's personal life anymore. She went back and found Youssef in a crowded hallway and handed him a letter. "Will you be the man to who's heart beat my heart dances and who places his hands on my cheek and ends all my storms?"

We sat at her parent's living room behind a partition so we could hear his official proposal to Hala's father. "I would be honored if you grant me your daughter's hand," he said and while Hala's father cleared his throat and prepared to answer he interrupted and said, "There is something I have to clarify."

"Go ahead," Hala's father said.

"My family cannot know about this marriage, they will never approve of Hala."

Hala jumped to her feet, knocked down the partition and told him to get out.

I comforted my friend for weeks then asked, "Hala, Ahmed hasn't married anyone else yet. What if he apologized, would you forgive him?"

"What would he say? Sorry? Isn't it strange that we believe a silly word like sorry could outweigh big words like dreams, expectations, hope, companionship, love, respect or dignity? I don't care if he apologizes a billion times. I've been alone since the day I married him and can be alone for the rest of my life."

Saeed came home to an insecure me and no longer rubbed his accomplishments in my face. Now he told me stories of women trying to race him on the street. Bumping into him in waiting lines. Coming into the office and telling him stories about their break ups. The woman who walked into the restaurant with nothing but leggings and a sports bra under her swung open Abaya and the butterfly tattoo on her stomach.

"Stop it!" I yelled. "Just stop now. We have a daughter upstairs, someday someone is going to talk about her the same way. Besides did it ever cross your mind that you are hurting my feelings. Do you know how many times I pretend not to see the single father trying to sit next to me when I take the kids to the gym? Or the car that follows me all the way home? Do you know how many times I pretend not to hear the guy trying to make conversation with me in a waiting room of a hospital? I never wave these things in your face it is disrespectful to you and me." Then, all the battles that never made it to the pages of our history popped up. "You would rather spend evenings with your friends than take me out, don't you think I ever need someone to tell me how beautiful I look. What kind of a marriage is this?" I broke down and cried. It wasn't a normal cry, it was a loud desperate cry for help.

He grabbed his keys and left the house, again!

Three days of silent treatment later I sent an apology text, again! He came home and greeted me with a hug like nothing had happened. I waited six months for Saeed to make a gesture, take me out, bring me flowers, send me a text anything. I got nothing. I decided it was time for me to move on and told Hala I would actually go with her and our other friends to that restaurant I always wanted to try out with him.

"I bet the food will taste just as good without him," she said.

"I feel like he's embarrassed to be seen with me in public," I whined in the car.

"I'm sure he is," she said.

"What!"

"Layla, all Saeed's friends are most likely at least a little conservative. I'm sure their wives wear the hijab if not cover their faces. He is not allowed to see any of them, and you want him to show you off with your uncovered hair and all?"

"I wish Saeed would at least once tell me he finds me beautiful, he has no problem noticing all the other women or speaking of them. I know it may sound ridiculous, but I feel like it's too soon for me to be fading away."

I hugged our friend Nora and congratulated her on her marriage and baby.

"Why didn't you come to the wedding?" one of her

sisters asked.

"I'm sorry, my husband was out of town and I couldn't find anyone to stay with the kids," I lied.

I didn't go to Nora's wedding because I had nothing to wear. Her wedding was right after my spring clean-up. I had given most of my dresses away and the ones I had left, everyone had seen me wear before. I was on my way to buy a new dress when Basheer, my fifty-six year old driver started to cry. "Madam please talk to boss. He will listen to you"

"Is this about you wanting to go on vacation? He told me already. He's right Basheer, you went two years in a row and promised not to go for another four years. You only get a holiday every two years it's in your contract."

"Madam, I'm not going on vacation. I have a court hearing. I will only be gone for five days I promise. Madam I have been working here for thirty years and every Riyal I made I sent to my father so he could buy and manage our farms. Now we need to register these lands again in a new electronic archive system all old documents will no longer be recognized. The government issued dates for each land owner, I missed one appointment and this is my next. If they cut off our power and water our harvest will rot. My father is too old to make the trip and the lands are in my name."

"I'll talk to him, I'm sure he'll let you go."

"No, he already allowed me to go. He just won't pay for my ticket."

"I'll pay for your ticket, just don't tell him."

"I'll pay you back Madam I promise."

"It's okay Basheer, you can pay me back on your own time."

I couldn't afford to buy a dress and Basheer's ticket. When I thought about it, Basheer was a closer friend to me than Nora. He had been with me every day for the last five years. He drove me around without ever complaining. He drove me to doctor's appointments when I was scared because Oday's fever won't go down or Maryam cut her chin open. He told them everything was going to be okay when I was too nervous to do so.

Basheer never judged my indecisiveness when he drove me back and forth five times to exchange a shirt. He knew which brand of yogurt I liked and brought me back some Parathas when he went out with his friends. He always brought us gifts when he came back from India. He pretended not to notice me weep in the back seat and patiently waited for me to wipe my tears and retouch my make up before opening the door. He smiled when he heard me laugh with the kids or my friends. He never wondered why I was repeatedly listening to the same song; he just enjoyed it with me. Standing by Basheer was more important than Nora's wedding. Besides I think the bride was too busy to notice I wasn't there and now she was happy she got to revisit that day and take me through every detail.

I tried to keep my eyes focused on Nora while she went on and on about her dress, the food, the music and flowers but they kept escaping to a woman behind her. She had an angelic face of someone who had never sinned. She wore a pale abaya and headscarf and no make-up. She looked so familiar I swear I have seen her before on many occasions but can't figure out where. She noticed me staring and smiled I smiled back thinking maybe she recognized me too. Halfway through our meal which was really good, Hala was right I don't think the food could have tasted any better with Saeed there. The woman walked toward us, picked a cushion off an empty couch and looked me straight in the eye. I was about to get up and shake her hand, still wondering where I knew her from when she smiled and said, "You know you are gorgeous. My friends and I couldn't help but notice how beautiful you are." I froze. I can't remember if I thanked her. I hope I get to see her again. I need to properly thank her and tell her how she saved me.

Without saying the words that strange woman told me that at the other end of the thread was not Saeed it was a whole Universe waiting to fulfill my every desire. I was just too focused on my husband to see it.

I was still beautiful. My daughter and her friends told me all the time. My presence was valued, my neighbor told me all the time. I was loved, my son said, "I love you" all the time. I may have not been honored with a noble prize, but my gardener named his first-born daughter after me. I was appreciated, my maid hugged me and told me I was the kindest human she knew.

Basheer never came back from that trip. I texted his daughter to ask about him she said his blood pressure and sugar levels were too high and he couldn't come back.

Almost four years later, he video called me. "Madam, I want to show you something," he happily announced with his whole family in the background.

"Basheer! How are you?" I asked.

"Look Madam, this is my land," he showed me a beautiful green landscape spread as far as the eye could see.

"And this is your house." He now showed me a small one story beige building. The same shade of beige as Saeed's house.

"What?"

"I told you I would pay you back Madam. Wait look inside, I found a bed like the one you were looking at in the furniture shop before you moved to the new house. Look, isn't it the same? Remember the one you told boss you loved but maybe he forgot. And this sofa, my son found a picture online and we had it custom made. This is your kitchen and bathroom and there are the children's rooms.

Don't cry Madam, this is your house we will take good care of it and you can come anytime you want. We have the papers ready this part of the land will be transferred to your name, Baba insists."

"Judy, can I ask you something?" I sat in the kitchen and asked my maid one day.

"Yes Madam."

"You've been here for so many years, you only go back home for a couple of months every two years. Where do you feel more at home, here or the Philippines?"

"You know the first time I came to Jeddah Madam, the first two weeks were exciting, the third week I became so homesick I called my mother and cried for hours every night. Just one more week. She would say to me, it takes a month for any place to become your home and she was right. Every time I started a new job, that's exactly how long it took me to feel at home and a month is how long it takes me to feel at home when I go back to the Philippines."

"What about the times you didn't like your employers?"

"Madam, the environment you're surrounded with is nothing but a gift. Sometimes the gift is a painting you love, which you frame and hang where everyone can see and admire. Other times the gift is an empty vase you find distasteful so you fill it with soil and a beautiful plant. Now you only admire the plant, and the vase is no longer visible. That's life," she said with a big smile.

My husband stood in front of me, his shoulders pushed back and chest popping out with a wide grin on his face. He started to tell me all about his latest adventure. The fluctuating pitch of his voice reminded of my sister when she came back from a party and gave my mother half-truths. "Jana and I made popcorn and tried out make up tutorials," she would say and my mother pretended to believe her.

I calmed myself down and silenced the noise. It was time for me to truly SEE this man. Not through the narrow lens of a film director trying to create a compilation of Bollywood romances, books written by relationship

experts and snippets from social media accounts but through my own eyes. I stripped this man from all that was me and looked at him. A boy who was raised in a segregated world. The only time he was allowed to openly compliment another was probably at his all boys' school when the boy at the desk next to him came in with new shoes. It must have gone down like this: "nice shoes" Saeed would say and the boy next to him would nod. They then became friends for life who exchanged a few words here and there but could always depend on each other. He was only expected to dress up and wear cologne when he was going to the mosque, an all men wedding party or a funeral. The only time he ecstatically danced the night away he was most likely surrounded by his male friends. He may have been a Layla's first love, rejected by her mother because of his last name or maybe a Layla was his first love and branded his heart not Abdullah. What about the times he went out of his way to buy his wife flowers for valentine's day and she did not buy him anything. Or when he took her on trips for their anniversary and she planned nothing. What about the times he whispered, you don't love me anymore but she was too busy changing diapers to hear him. The times he wanted to hold her a second longer, but she ran to pick the kids up from school. All the times she did not pretend to laugh at his joke or get jealous when he spoke about other women but instead dragged their daughter into the conversation. He never watched that Bollywood movie that seduced me into marriage. He never promised to travel across continents for me. Hell, he never promised to travel across the living room for me. He did not promise to break free of the grip of twenty men to wipe my tears or place the stars at my feet. He made me one promise, to double my salary if I stayed home and he kept that promise. Even when it meant he got no sick days, even through a global economic crisis and a pandemic he kept his promise.

Free from all the imaginary walls I created, I saw that Saeed loved me as much as I loved him and just because he believed he saved me it did not mean he was going to hurt me. I allowed myself and him to BE in our final resting place.

Maybe it is time to ask Why?

Why do we restrict our desires to titles, relationships and faces? Why do we seek discipline from our father's yet hate our mothers for being strict? Why do we expect our mother's to be fragile but refuse to brace our fathers? Why do we respect every silly rule created by our grandfathers yet challenge the law? No freedom is limitless, so why then, are you a law-abiding citizen and I oppressed? why does it matter that my rules look different than yours, or that my people decide to change at a different time than yours? Why do we miss resting our head on our grandmother's lap but resist with every breath to sit on her chair? Why do we expect our spouses to fill the voids we ourselves dug into our soul? Why do we believe it is our job to make our children better people and not the other way around?

What if we freed our desires from the shackles of title, face and place and allowed what we seek to find its way to us.

What if you and I were not small entities dropped into a linear complex of time, expected to play the roles we are entangled in? What if time was nothing but a tool we invented to keep us organized? What if God created you and for you he created a Universe? What if you were the center of the Universe that comes into existence with your awareness and will disappear with it? What if the people in our lives were sent to teach us?

I was given a grandfather to teach me that man's biggest strength was resilience and even the strongest of men can fail to discipline his own ego.

A grandmother to teach me that detachment did not entail renouncing the worldly and hiding in a cave or posting about my introverted self on social media. It meant dinners at an eighteen seater table with a subtle smile because I was untouched by the madness. It meant being able to see the guilty eyes of your loved ones and stroke their hair without judgement. It meant crocheting for hours without the need to show your creation to anyone.

I was given a mother to teach me how easy it is to

misunderstand the person who loves you the most.

My father taught me that sometimes the wars we don't initiate or fight are the ones that leave us defeated and sometimes that one battle makes all others seem pointless.

God gave me a friend, Hala. A mirror to show me all that I'm not and all that I am capable of. It's a pity we limit our tolerance and altruism to those we call our friends and no one else.

He gave me siblings to teach me that the world is not fair. Not everyone is given the same opportunities but I still got to where I wanted to be.

Ummi to teach me that beauty is not in the eye of the beholder but a dance to a song that comes from the heart and strength is not in a stare or flexed bicep but the ability to be a village for your neighbor.

Judy took on most of my responsibilities allowing me the freedom to explore life. She showed me that everything was happening here and now.

Basheer revealed to me that a home is not a piece of paper with your name on it; it is not in the color of paint or the number of bricks; it is not in the mother land of your father or where your mother was born. It is where life happens because you exist.

God gave us the power to manifest the perfect partner. That person he created to complete us, to selflessly do all that needed to be done for our lives to be whole. If only we trusted him as much as we believed the Media.

My children remind me that all I have to leave them is the whole world. I pray we change in time to leave them a better one.